History of an Executioner

Clancy
McGilligan

History of an Executioner

Miami University Press

Library of Congress Cataloging-in-Publication Data

Names: McGilligan, Clancy, author.

Title: History of an executioner / by Clancy McGilligan.

Description: Oxford, Ohio : Miami University Press, [2019]

Identifiers: LCCN 2019023785 | ISBN 9781881163664 (trade paperback)

Classification: LCC PS3613.C4825 H57 2019 | DDC 813/.6—dc23

LC record available at https://lccn.loc.gov/2019023785

Designed by Crisis

Printed on acid-free, recycled paper

in the United States of America

Miami University Press

356 Bachelor Hall

Miami University

Oxford, Ohio 45056

History
of an
Executioner

She is awake when I open my eyes and has moved from our bed to her chair. I am not surprised. Since her fall, she spends the days sitting and looking out the window. The view is pleasant enough, I guess, but it is not worth the time she devotes to it. All you can see is the road winding between wheat fields, the reddish-brown roofs of town in the distance, the humps of the hills farther east.

I rise and make the bed, spreading the blanket evenly over the mattress. It is important to be tidy in so small a house. Then I greet her. She shifts her head but does not turn around.

From the table I lift the large ceramic bowl that covers what remains of yesterday's loaf, protecting it from field mice and cockroaches. I cut two slices for myself and one for her. I sit at the table and wait for my mind to clear, chewing slowly. She looks out one window, and I look out the other. The sun has not risen above the line of the hills.

When I try to draw her out, she ignores me and nibbles at her slice of bread. Her skirt has caught on the chair, and I can see one of her pale thighs. I find her more attractive these days, but I am a little ashamed of this. Also, I do not understand it. She has lost some of the plumpness in her face, but nothing else about her has changed: her thick black hair has the same amount of gray, her chin juts out like a small fist, her cheeks have kept their blotchiness. She is nearly a decade older than me.

"Do you want to go for a walk today?" I ask. Exercise might help restore her to her old self, and I am willing to endure some of her scorn if it does. "Lena?"

"No," she says, and shakes her head to make sure I understand.

I wait until the sun is in the sky. Then I collect the prisoner from the jail. A soldier and I escort him to the square. It is hot, with the wind stirring up dust in the streets, and soon the prisoner requests a drink. We knock on a door in town and an old woman answers, offering us a jug and a single cup. The soldier drinks first. Afterward he passes the cup to the prisoner and the woman refills it. I can tell from the way she eyes me that she does not want me to drink, that she will probably throw out the cup if I use it, so I do not ask for it. I am used to this kind of treatment. Then the prisoner offers me the cup anyway. I shake my head. I appreciate his kindness, but I hope he does not think it will change anything. I am not unfeeling, but I learned long ago to block emotion when it comes to prisoners. Farmers must do the same with the cows they slaughter. Maybe they have a harder time because they raise the animals from birth.

What the prisoner says afterward is unusual. As we continue

walking, he talks to me about how horrible it is to die in town. He speaks in the dialect of the hills, but I can make out his meaning. He says he cannot stand the straight walls and streets. The roofs that hide the sun and stars. The people, so many people, so close. The absence of animals and trees and grass. Or the smell. How do people die, much less live, in a place like this? he asks. And what will we do with his body?

I do not answer the first question. I tell him his body will be buried out of town, on a hillside, in the graveyard for criminals.

I am no criminal, he says.

The rebels are treated as criminals, I explain, because the soldier remains quiet. That is why I execute them.

But I am no rebel, he says. He tells me he was arrested while shepherding his flock with his sons. A patrol of soldiers accused him of supplying the rebels with milk and meat. He claims this is nonsense, that there are no rebels left near him, that the Republic's forces killed them all years ago.

The soldier interrupts with jeers at this point.

When we come to the paved town square, I lead him up the stairs to the wooden platform, three or so feet off the ground. I think I see someone in a window on the fourth floor of the town hall, where the town manager's office is. The soldier crouches in the shade of an olive tree on the east side of the square, in front of the church, with one hand on his upright musket. Nearby stand a group of children and a candied almond vendor.

After the prisoner kneels at the heavy wooden block in the center of the platform, I undo his shackles and tie each hand to a metal ring sticking out of the wood. Then I tell him to lay his face in the hollow.

He does not beg or whimper. But after I raise my axe, and before I drive the blade into the stained wood, he turns slightly and looks at me out of the corner of his right eye.

The following day, the jailer seems to be waiting for me when I enter the gate. He rises from his seat on the bench against the wall of his house, in the corner of the courtyard near the garrison. Then he crosses to the cells and announces over his shoulder that there are to be no more executions. He pretends to inspect the cell bars. I wonder if I have misheard him.

"There must be some mistake," I say.

He smiles and approaches, looking up at me because I am much taller. "There has been an uproar in the capital," he says. "Over a careless execution."

"Careless?"

He takes a few steps back. "They needed ten blows to separate a stubborn head."

I will admit things like that are possible. But I have only ever needed one blow. "The executioner must have been inexperienced," I say.

"While the head lay on the ground," he continues, "someone slapped one of the cheeks, and the eyes blinked." His halo of gray, frizzy hair shakes as he laughs. "I understand that the audience included certain legislators. Afterward, Parliament voted to halt all death sentences around the country. They want to consider the matter."

"Consider what?"

"I'm not sure, exactly," he says. "You need to speak with the town manager."

It dawns on me why he is gloating. He receives an allowance for each prisoner, and he only needs a small part of that for food. No executions means more prisoners at the jail, means more money for him.

He sits beside his boy on the bench. I wait for him to speak again, but after a while he rises and enters the garrison, passing through the doorway in the wall that divides the compound. Maybe he thinks I need time to understand. Like everyone else, he seems to believe that because I talk slowly, I also think slowly.

His boy does not follow but watches me with his closely set eyes. I turn toward the cells and realize the two prisoners must have heard everything.

I have no idea what I will do if there are no more executions.

Leaving the jail, I wander to the stream that runs through town and follow it west until the houses end and I reach the small waterfall. I sit by the shallow pool, among the roots of a cottonwood, so I can think. Small black ants crawl under and around and sometimes over me. One wanders onto my thigh. I flick it with my fingers and it arcs into the water. I feel a little bad about that, and afterward I let them climb on me.

It is a shame they botched the execution in the capital. I have never been there and do not know how they do things. Probably it is similar, though I guess they still have an audience. These days, although we go past the inn, and past the market where Lena used to sell herbs, few people stop to watch, and only children come to the square. Prisoners started arriving regularly some seven years ago, when Parliament passed the special powers act. After so many executions, people have lost interest. Nobody cares about another shepherd accused of feeding rebels, another rebel found disguised as a farmer.

The next thing I know, the light is fading. I rise and follow the stream back toward town. As I walk, I see a group of gray shapes moving in my direction on the opposite bank. At first I think it is a pack of mules, but then I make out the outlines of children, maybe boys. There are many of them, ten or fifteen.

As we near each other, they cross onto my bank, splashing carelessly through the narrow stream.

I continue along the water's edge, guessing they will take the outer part of the path. But they move closer and I pass in the middle of them. Most barely reach my chest, and I do not pay much attention until I feel something hit my shoulder. Then more objects, pebbles I think, strike my back and sides. They are having some fun with me, I realize. But the pebbles hardly hurt. I push a few boys away and keep walking. One says something about executions. Then a stone strikes the back of my head and my anger takes over. I swing out with my arm. When I look down, the boys are huddled together, their backs to me. I move closer and see, at their center, one bleeding from his head. I must have hit him. There is yelling, and a few of the bigger boys pick up their injured friend and hurry back to town, followed by the others.

I hope I did not badly hurt the boy. I was only defending myself, though maybe I should not have done so. They are only children.

I wait a while, then continue along the stream and take back streets through town until I reach the road home.

Lena is in her chair, and I see there is only a heel of bread left. I forgot to visit one of the bakers, and now it is too late. I give her the bread and some tomato. I do not tell her what has happened.

I stay in bed most of the next morning, throwing off the blanket when the heat gathers strength and I begin to sweat. The house seems smaller, the wooden floor dirtier.

Lena sits as usual in her chair. She has moved again from the bed when she woke. She has made no sign she is hungry.

I should speak with the town manager. Instead I take out the book my father got on one of his trips across the southern provinces, when being the executioner meant traveling from place to place. He taught me to read, telling me I needed to be smarter than the people in town. As far as I can tell, few of them recognize more than numbers. Lena, for example, only understands a few words. She liked to say reading would dry out my brain.

The red spine and cover are so worn that the letters have disappeared, and the beginning pages are missing. Above the first chapter heading, *Histories of the New World* is written in a neat hand. Opening the book, I read of a strange game. Organized once a month and lasting for days, this game was controlled by priests who lived apart from the rest of the population. At the start, they hid a sacred fruit in a large territory of forest and swamps, with a staff as a marker. The players then tried to find and bring the fruit to a temple without having it taken away. The winner ate this prize. Produced through special farming methods, the fruit supposedly allowed the eater to speak with the gods, though sometimes it also caused death. The book says its skin was hairy like a coconut's, while its flesh was soft and purple. When foreigners came and conquered the land, the priests rooted out and completely destroyed the plant.

I have read the book many times, puzzling out the words my father never taught me. The people live on a "bight," for example, while the priests are a "caste." My guess is that "bight" has something to do with the sea. I have never seen the sea, but as far as I can tell it surrounds the New World. “Caste” must be a special group of some kind, maybe chosen by someone like the town manager.

One of the things I like about this game is that everyone plays. Everyone but the priests, that is. Sometimes I imagine myself wandering through the forest as I search for the prize, followed by a priest. Then eating the fruit, and a sense of rising up, out of things.

After reading for a while longer, I put the book back in the chest. I walk outside, slipping on my sandals, and shuffle among the rows of Lena’s garden.

The tarragon plants are tall enough now that I can run my hands over their feathery leaves without bending down. The basil, lower to the ground, is a deep green. I can see it is time to harvest and sell some of the herbs, but Lena has stopped paying attention to them.

I lower a pail into the well and bring it back up, then empty it into the watering can. I douse the plants, going up and down the rows, as I do every few days now.

At the edge of our land, I look down the gentle slope at the stubble of the surrounding fields and the piles of harvested wheat and then at the town in the distance.

I must go see the town manager.

×

I stand in the center of the reception room. There are two chairs against the wall behind me, one on either side of the window that faces the square, but they are too fine for me to sit on.

The slender assistant appears in the doorway to the office. He gives me a curious look, though more than an hour ago he told me to wait in this very spot. The town manager is talking inside. He has a deep, impressive voice.

The assistant disappears.

A full bookcase stands against the wall in front of me. From my position, I cannot quite make out the titles on the spines. It would be nice to have another book or two, or at least to be able to read another, but the town manager would never give me one, I am sure of that.

Finally the town manager, Tronk, enters. He fixes his small brown eyes on me.

"I am glad you came," he says. "You must have heard."

I nod.

He smooths the sheet of hair on his neck. "It must be difficult to understand, living as you do outside our town. You do live outside town?"

I nod again.

"So far from the heart of our Republic. To be sure, I am far, too." He laughs. "But I have my friends in the capital, my informants and allies." Another laugh. "Let me cut to the heart of the matter. What it comes down to, in my view, is that we are in a new age, that there is a radical thinking afoot. Certain prominent persons—prominent, from *pro* and *minere*, let's remember, to project a threat—certain prominent persons, you see, feel our executions contradict the spirit of the times. They believe them cruel. *Inhumane*, they call them." He steps closer. His breath smells of red meat. "The question is, I think, not whether something is cruel, but whether it is too cruel for the spirit of the times." He smiles. "In other words: is something with or against this spirit? Are you, for example? In the Republic, we must all move in step."

"What will happen next?" I ask, wanting him to move away.

He steps back. His platform shoes make rapping sounds on the patterned woodwork of the floor.

"There are to be no more executions for now."

"For now?"

"Yes, for now."

"How long is that for?"

"How long?" He seems to be thinking about something else. "They have not said. But they are considering—they are debating—they are trying to decide whether to completely end executions. That is what is wanted by these extremists."

It still seems hard to believe that they can end executions, just like that.

"I have personally assured my contacts," he continues, "that you, at least, have never failed to dispatch a prisoner with the utmost alacrity and kindness, given the circumstances—yes, I used the word 'kindness.' But there is nothing to be done now except wait. The stay is in place."

"But what will happen to me?"

"To you?"

"I mean, what about my pay?"

"Pay?" He chuckles. "*Pacare*—to pacify, make peaceful." He moves behind me and gazes out the window. I remain facing forward, trying not to upset him. Once I got him worked up and he began scolding me for not knowing the history of the Republic, though I had only asked him why executions needed to be held in the square. The scolding turned into a kind of lesson, and soon enough a few hours had gone by. "Well," he says finally, "they haven't said anything about the executioners, only the executions. I suppose that means you'll keep your position for the moment and collect your pay as usual. This is technically only a temporary stay, remember. Parliament sometimes makes noises one way, then goes the other. It's impossible to say what will happen, really. Although, the way things seem, I wouldn't be surprised if they make it permanent." He moves backward. "Don't look so unhappy—the government always does best. In any event, you still have your salary for now."

That night, I wake to find Lena on top of me. She has removed her shirt, and the tops of her shoulders seem to reflect the moonlight from the open windows. My body responds to hers, and in my drowsy state I think nothing of her sudden interest in me.

She puts me inside her. She presses her breasts against my chest, digs her face into my neck. Then I feel it. A bite on my neck, though it draws no blood. I ask her what she is doing, but she does not answer. Instead she bites me again, now on my chin, her front teeth grinding for a moment against bone. I say nothing this time. For some reason I am sure she will not stop. She moves higher and turns her face sideways. As she leans in, I realize what she intends to do, and it is then that she snaps her mouth down, clamping her teeth onto the tip of my nose. With her mouth still closed she pulls back, and I hear a tearing sound.

I wake and see the back of her head above the foot of the bed. She is in her chair. I feel my nose. It is still whole. A dream.

From the light coming through the windows, I guess it is past noon. I never sleep this late.

I go to the well and dump a pail of cold water over my head. My erection pushes against my underwear despite my memory of the tearing sound. As I walk back inside, I try to hide it in case Lena turns around. I keep from looking at her.

After lying on the bed, I consider making my daily visit to the jail. But then I remember the stay, I remember that there is no point in visiting the jail anymore.

My erection fails to go away. I glance at Lena. Since her sickness, we have only had intercourse in my dreams, and it is not like before. For one, sometimes in the dreams we are in the garden, and once we were at the market. But also, wherever we are, she bites me, or screams into my ear, or drags her nails across my back and chest until I bleed. I dislike the dreams, but when I wake I cannot help thinking about her body, about undressing her. I know that, even though she might not object, I should not do this. I know that in her condition she is not interested.

There is something else I have considered, something to free me of these thoughts. Lena does not need to know. I lie in bed thinking. Finally I take some money from a hole in the wall that I plug with a piece of plaster. I tell her I am going to the baker's shop she favored, the one on the far side of town.

The brothel sits on a hummock beside the hills, north of the stream and south of the graveyard. I pass it whenever I fetch a cart and bring a body for the gravedigger, but I have never been inside.

It is a normal stucco house, but very large, and with no exterior decoration. When I enter, I find myself in a dim room with couches against the walls. Two men sit on the couches. Not knowing what to do, I sit down too. I do not recognize them, and I wonder if they know me, if they will leave now that I am here. But one looks at me and smiles.

A bald man with a beard pokes his head through a curtained doorway and politely asks me to wait. Soon he returns and gestures to one of the men to follow him. He comes back and does the same for the second. I am not there long before he signals for me.

The man introduces himself as Bersil, the master of the house. He treats me like someone important and brings me to a room where six women in light-colored pajamas play cards around a table. When I enter they stand and look at me with what I take to be curiosity. The man tells me their names and where they are from, but his voice is drowned out by a humming in my head. When I remain quiet, he describes their specializations. I tell him one has caught my eye.

She is tall, unlike Lena, although she has the same black hair. Her long neck seems to narrow toward the base of her head. When I look more closely, I see that her posture is a little crooked. I cannot decide if it is only the way she stands, or if one of her legs is longer than the other.

After I pay, we go in silence to a room on the second floor. Inside she opens the slats of the two windows to let in more light.

"What do you want?" she asks.

"Let's lie together on the bed," I say. I don't remember her specialization, or anything the master of the house said about her. "What's your name?"

"Emmer," she says. We lie side by side on our backs.

"What does it mean?"

"It doesn't mean anything." She fidgets.

"Do you know who I am?"

"Are you someone important?"

"I'm just the executioner."

She says nothing.

"Does that bother you?" I ask.

"Why should it bother me? It has nothing to do with me."

I am glad about that. Lena often said unpleasant things about my position. We are silent for a while. I hear her stomach growl, a low rumbling that must last for five whole seconds.

"Are you hungry?" I ask.

"No. Sometimes my stomach makes noises. Does it spoil your mood?"

"It's fine." Then I add, feeling braver, "Maybe you can undress now."

She stands and slips off her pajamas and then her underclothes. They are different from Lena's, with lace edges, and look uncomfortable. Once her clothes are off, her body straightens, her eyes grow bold, her lips turn at the corners into a smile.

"Are you disappointed?" she asks.

I shake my head. "Will you lie down again?"

"What do you want?"

"I'm not sure."

"This is your first time here."

I nod.

"Then let me decide."

Lena was energetic in bed when we first married, though only at first. Emmer is not really like that. Though she moans softly, each of her movements seems calm and thought out, as if she were only completing a household task. At first I feel awkward with her, but then I reflect that I have experience of only one other woman and should not let my expectations get in the way of things. And so I start to enjoy myself, and soon we are both sweating, and her eyelids flutter a little. When I climax, it is with an intensity new to me, as if something has been forced open inside me.

Afterward she leads me back to the room with the other women. As we walk, I tell her I will visit her again. I cannot help chattering in my excitement. She laughs but I know her laugh is friendly. I know that she laughs with me, that we have just shared something.

Outside I walk around the corner to the brothel's south wall. The view strikes me as especially beautiful. To my left brown hills climb toward huge white clouds that seem pinned to the sky. Between the hills, the stream turns and disappears and reappears until it shoots out among a stand of trees and rushes along the plain to town, passing through the reeds near the brothel.

I can hear the wind coming off the hills and the occasional opening and closing of the door around the corner as customers come and go.

Somehow the hours pass, and when next I look west the sun sits low in the sky. I stumble out from against the wall. As I pass the front door, a man comes out. He is short, with a head of wild white hair. I realize he is the jailer just as he recognizes me. He speaks first.

"Did you have some fun?" he asks.

"Isn't it always fun?"

I think there is something in my reply that knocks down, in one blow, the barrier between us, but maybe he is only happy from his visit. In any case, he smiles and suggests we go to the inn for a drink. Though I do not drink I say yes. I am happy and do not want to go home yet.

We walk for the most part in silence, stopping on the way at the baker's so I can buy a loaf. When we enter the inn, two men seated at the counter give me a curious look. The jailer moves to a booth in the corner and I follow, setting my loaf on the table. A man in an apron appears from a back room. He asks what we want, coldly. The jailer, ignoring his manner, orders a carafe of wine.

"Wine is best afterward," he says when the man leaves. "Beforehand it ruins your breathing and endurance, or at least mine. One glass leads to two glasses, and two to three, and that is too many."

I nod. "I don't drink wine very often."

"I thought so. You don't seem like a drinker. A good drink

every once in a while restores you, makes you see everything with fresh eyes. It's like a visit to the brothel." He smiles. "Who did you have?"

It occurs to me then that we may have both slept with Emmer. The thought fills me with disgust. I imagine the jailer naked, his belly hanging down and almost covering his genitals. I would rather Emmer be mine alone, though I know that this is impossible, even ridiculous, given her position.

"I cannot remember her name," I tell him.

"What did she look like?"

I describe one of the other women I saw playing cards: small with red hair, pale skin, a snub nose.

"Ah, Ray. I know her well. Did she do her trick? Where she bends backward, into a bridge?"

I nod, wondering what that looks like. "Who did you see?"

"Jana. She's the only one I go to these days."

I feel a wave of relief, though I know he may have slept with Emmer before, that many have slept with her before.

The man in the apron brings the carafe of red wine and two glasses, and the jailer pours. I drink. My body grows pleasantly hot. The wine does not taste as bad as I remember. The night Lena and I were married, I had a glass and became sick. I have not tried any since then.

"Jana and I play a game. Do you want to hear about it?" he asks. He has already emptied his glass and pours himself another.

I nod.

"She pretends she's the jailer, and I pretend I'm her. Strange, isn't it?"

I am not sure whether to agree. I clear my throat.

"This is a fantasy of mine," he continues. "I can't explain it."

I wonder why he is telling me this. "What does she do?"

"She orders me around."

"Is that all?"

"And we do the rest. You think it sounds foolish?"

"No, that isn't it." Images come to me of the jailer taking orders from this Jana: I see him bending down, dancing, rubbing her feet. I stop myself from smiling. He watches me as I take a careful drink of my wine. "I was only trying to understand," I add.

"How about you? What do you do?"

"I don't have a routine."

"You must do something special."

"I mean, nothing like that."

"You must drink faster," he says, frowning. "You don't know how it's done."

I drink despite the feeling that the wine is unbalancing me.

One of the men at the counter stands and approaches our booth with a hunched-over posture.

"I've seen you before," he says to me.

I look closely at him. He appears drunk. "No, you are mistaken," I tell him.

He pauses. "Are you saying you're not who I think you are?"

Under his glare, I surrender. "Sorry, you're right."

"And do you think we," he gestures to the lone man at the counter, "want to drink and eat with you?"

I say nothing, merely return his gaze. His square face hovers above me like a blunt weapon.

"It is clean work," I mumble.

"Clean? What's clean about it? Let me see."

He grabs my hands. When I feel his rough skin, I push him away. He stumbles back and regains his balance. Then, after hesitating, he returns to the counter. Out of the corner of my eye, I notice the man in the apron watching from the back room.

"There you go!" says the jailer to me. "Stand your ground!"

He raises his glass and I drink with him, and my head feels like it is burning, but I cannot tell if it is from the wine or from embarrassment at being made the center of attention, at being identified aloud as the executioner.

"There is nothing to be done about it, you know," the jailer continues. His face is a deep red.

"About what?"

"You'll always be treated like that in town. That's the way people feel. They are simple people, and why would they change their minds."

"What about you?"

"I'm the same, but I have gotten to know you a little, and I see that you are a simple person, too. But now I wonder: what will you do?"

"What do you mean?"

"What else?"

I do not reply right away. "I am still the executioner."

"But there will be no more executions!"

"It has not been decided. I spoke to the town manager."

A burp escapes him. "That's just a formality. Think about it. What I say is, you are still young. Why don't you go somewhere else?"

"I am not young."

"Young enough. There's always a need for executioners somewhere. Across the sea, in the New World, for example. Have you considered that?"

The New World. I have not considered it. "What about my wife? She's sick."

"Maybe she will get better there."

Three soldiers enter and sit at the bar. I recognize one of them. The jailer drains his third glass. My head has begun to throb, and I have the frightening feeling that my mind and body are no longer completely my own, that I have lost control over myself.

"Think about it," he says. "I will give you a good price for your land. Do you want this?"

I shake my head and he takes my glass and drinks. So, he wants my land. But is going to the New World such a bad idea?

The man in the apron approaches. "Can you pay the bill?" he asks.

The jailer turns toward him a moment, then downs the rest of my glass. "We were just leaving," he says and looks at me.

I can tell he wants me to pay, and so I reach in my pocket. But then I see myself at the table with the jailer as if from across the room, and I feel disgusted with both of us, with how red we are, with the jailer's satisfied face and my own willingness to please him, and the force of it all stops me from taking out any money.

The jailer coughs once, twice, bringing me back to the moment, and the feeling leaves me. I should be the one to pay. The jailer was kind enough to invite me. I pass some coins to the man, but he tells me they are not enough. I give him another. One of the soldiers leans toward his companions and gestures at us, laughing.

The sun is setting when we step outside, and I smell beef stew simmering in the inn kitchen. My mouth waters as we walk up the road together, but I do not eat any of the loaf I bought earlier. The jailer talks, mostly to himself, about his plans to expand his house in the jail. Twice he stumbles and falls, and when I help him up he only curses me. He does not say goodbye when we part at the crossing. I watch him zigzagging down the road. I do not care if he falls and hurts himself. At home I devour half the loaf of bread. Lena only takes a few bites of a slice, though she has not eaten all day. When I ask her, a little guiltily, if she enjoyed her day, she says nothing more than her name. I am not sure what she means.

I lie on the bed, bloated and tired, my stomach queasy from the wine. I think of my trip to the brothel. I may have betrayed Lena by going there, but she is sick. I can still do my duty to her.

×

That night I do not dream, or do not remember any dreams. I wake at sunrise and figure that, with my savings and salary, I can afford to visit Emmer once a week. The thought makes me giddy, and I pace around the bed. Lena, already awake, sits in her chair, her back to me. She has become more and more withdrawn these last few weeks. I do not remember her coming to bed last night.

"It is not so bad, this town," I say. She does not show she has heard. "But it's true that, two days ago, I learned the government has stopped all the executions."

She draws herself up a little. "Always?" she asks without turning around, and it takes me a moment to understand her meaning. "Always," along with "Lena" and "no," seem to be the only words she can say since her fall.

"Just for a while," I reply. "The government is thinking about making it permanent." This makes me pause. I see her shift slightly to look at me and then turn back toward the window. I go on: "I can guess what you would say: 'What will you do now?' I don't know. But at least I'm still to be paid my salary."

I wait. She continues to look out the window.

"You always disliked my position. You even asked me not to mention it. I haven't forgotten. All I could talk about with you was the latest gossip from the market: who the wife of the pear seller ran away with, or why a tailor was spreading lies about a soldier from the garrison. I never understood why I should care what happens to those people. But I guess you did not really care. You only wanted it to seem like you did."

I wait but still she looks out the window. Maybe I am being cruel to her. She is sick, and I should not make her days unpleasant. I pace in silence for a while.

"You must want to know why I am in such a good mood, despite the news. Well, last night I went to the inn with the jailer. He has become friendly with me. We drank two carafes of wine and I did not feel sick at all. I think I have a taste for it now."

The lie, the small revision of what happened the night before, is unplanned. I decide to go on.

"You might like to hear something the jailer told me. He is thinking of leaving with his boy for the New World. He says that running a jail is no longer as profitable as it used to be. He says there must be plenty of prisoners across the sea. What do you think of that?"

I look down at her as I pass the chair. She has the same blank expression.

"It is a risk," I continue, "that is true. But sometimes I wonder about the New World, about what it offers." I glance at her again.

"No," she says, and shakes her head for emphasis, or to make her feelings clear, because she also uses "no" to mean "yes."

"Anyway, I thought you might like to hear some news from town."

I keep pacing, then stop at the table and look out the window, so that she is sitting in front of one window, and I am standing in front of the other. Finally I cut some bread for us.

After we eat, I tell her, "I should go to the jail to see if there has been any news. Parliament may have voted to end the stay."

×

The soldier on duty lies awake in a hammock strung between a cottonwood and a metal ring driven into the jail's outside wall. When I walk into the courtyard, the jailer and his boy are nowhere to be seen. The prisoners watch me from their seats on the dirt floor of their cell. The one with a missing ear, named Ear by the boy, motions for me to come closer. The grimy pink spiral where his ear should be is there for all to see. The jailer claimed he lost it in one of the rituals of the people who farm the tableland beyond the hills, but I wonder if it was cut off by the soldiers.

He rises. "What will happen now that the executions are finished?" he asks. The other prisoner, named Two by the boy, remains seated. I can smell the contents of the pail used as a toilet in a corner. Flies buzz around the metal rim, landing and taking off and going down inside. "Will I be freed?" Ear asks. He shifts his head slightly as if to let me have a better look, and I stare at the pink root system in the side of his head. "We have helped. We have provided the names of other rebels."

"I don't know anything about that. What did the jailer say?"

"He tells us nothing. Please, we are only farmers."

I think for a moment. "Then how did you know the names of other rebels?"

He shrugs. "It's not hard to come up with a few names."

I glance at Two. When the flies travel to his side of the cell and land on his head or face, he slowly lifts his hand to swat them away. His eyelids are half closed.

"What's wrong with him?" I ask.

A shout from behind me interrupts our conversation. I turn and see the jailer standing outside his house with his boy.

"Why are you here?" he demands.

"One of the prisoners is sick."

"As if I didn't know that." He scowls, the warmth he showed at the inn gone. "What do you want?"

"I came to check if there has been any news."

"There has been no news. What do you expect? It's only been a few days."

I do not answer.

"If there's something, I will send the boy for you. There's no need for you to keep coming." He kicks at the dirt and seems to want to say something else, but instead waves the back of his hand to dismiss me. He goes back into his house.

So this is how it will be: I am no longer welcome at the jail. At least I have Emmer.

The boy does not follow his father inside, but stays where he is, watching me. He is always watching. His father is training him to run the jail, as my father taught me to handle an axe. I cannot tell if the boy enjoys the work. Maybe he does not need to. I do not know if I enjoy mine, exactly. But I take pride in doing it well.

After a moment he takes something out of his pocket, then moves forward and holds it up for me to see. It is made of two wooden discs attached at the center, with a string coming out of the space in between. It fits neatly in his palm.

"What is that?" I ask.

He runs his middle finger along an edge, slipping it into a loop at the end of the string. Then, with a flick of his wrist, he sends the two discs shooting down together along the string. After reaching the end, they return to his palm with a hissing sound. I watch as he repeats the trick. But the third time he tries it, the discs separate and fall to the dirt instead of coming back. I see one has a short peg that fits into a hole in the other. He kneels and picks up the two pieces.

"I need to glue it together," he says.

"Where did you get it?"

"I made it." He ties the string around the peg and puts the discs back together.

"It's a clever toy."

"It's not only a toy."

"What else does it do?"

"Nothing."

I nod, not wanting to argue.

"Do you want to try?" he asks, brushing a lock of hair out of his eyes.

I shake my head. I doubt I have the skill to do such a trick. "What will happen to the prisoners now?" I ask.

"They will be prisoners, like before." He smiles at his reply. "What do you care?"

I look back at Ear and Two and decide that it has nothing to do with me. I walk toward the gate.

"They are looking for you," he calls after me.

I stop and turn.

"You hit a boy on the head," he says.

I remember when the group of boys attacked me by the stream. "What happened to him?"

The jailer's boy strolls to the cells. Ear moves backward, and so does Two, but more slowly. After reaching the bars, he swivels on one foot so he faces me, then tosses his toy into the air and catches it. "He lay in bed for a day or so. Now he's fine."

Though I forgot about the boy, the last thing I want is to have hurt him. "His parents are angry with me?"

"His parents? They don't know. He and his friends lied to them. But the gang have vowed to find you and take revenge. The oldest said he's going to put you in bed with a rock to your head." As he talks, he fits the loop on a finger and sends the toy downward. This time it comes back. "Are you worried?"

I do not answer him. Few townspeople venture into the countryside. The boys must not know where I live. I imagine them roaming the town, keeping an eye out for me. But I am not scared of children.

"If you'd like, I can talk to them for you," he says. "I know you aren't too quick." He taps his head. "You probably didn't mean any harm. In any case, they are stupid boys. They deserved anything you did to them."

"I did not want to hurt him," I say. Then I turn and walk through the gate. The soldier is asleep now on the hammock, though it is still morning. I look up toward the sun and am momentarily blinded.

"Alright then," the boy calls after me. "I'll talk to them for you. But you owe me a favor!"

I do not look back. I walk down the main road for a while, then cut through the back roads until I reach the stream. I follow it west. Soon the houses end and I come to the pool beneath the small waterfall. I pause and rest. When I hear voices on the path from town, I go on. Ten minutes later I turn south for a series of rock outcroppings in a wheat field. The stand of trees downstream hides the house of the man who farms the land, and I do not see him or anyone else. I scale the largest of the outcroppings, a gray ball of stone jutting fifteen feet out of the ground, and go down the other side. I continue toward the low hills in the distance.

Before long the jailer's boy and even the executions seem unimportant. A good walk clears my mind and lets me forget the unpleasantness in my life. Though I like the birds and the trees and the grass, I think it is because of the rhythm, the repetition of one step and then another. After a while my body takes over and my mind disappears, so that there is only what I am doing and nothing else. Sometimes I take as many as three walks a day. I stay out of the hills to the east, where they say the rebels live, and I do not go far south or north of town. Mostly I go west.

When I reach the top of a low hill, I turn to take in the town and everything else. I stand there for a while. From that point of view, it seems as if the world is either much bigger or much smaller than I thought.

Before I go home, I visit the small grocery. The shop is shuttered when I arrive. Only then do I notice the silence in town. It is midday, when people rest. I lean against the wall, in the shade, to wait.

The grocery has fewer things for sale than the market, but it is less busy and closer to home. It is also where I met Lena. She worked there for many years. At first she acted like everyone else, but as time went on she began to joke with me or find an excuse to bump into me. Then one day she suggested we marry. That was a surprise, but a good one. My father had encouraged me to find a wife. Lena told me afterward she did not want children, that it was hard enough to care for ourselves. She called ours a "convenience marriage," explaining that she needed to free herself of the grocer. He adopted her when she was an orphan but did not treat her well, and he demanded I pay him to marry her because, he said, he would be losing a worker. When I remember such things, I feel sorry for Lena. She has had a difficult life, as she used to remind me.

After a while the grocer opens the door and windows, and I request five pounds of onions and three of tomatoes. Though he knows Lena is sick, he does not ask about her.

As he gathers the food, I notice hanging strips of salted cod against the back wall.

"Where is that from?" I ask.

It takes him a moment to understand what I'm talking about. "The sea. Where else?"

"Which sea?"

"Does it matter?"

The cod is expensive, but I decide to treat Lena and myself. That night we eat the fish with tomato and bread and a little oil.

I tear off a strip for her, then a strip for me. As she chews she slowly draws up the stringy flesh until it disappears between her lips. She does not say anything, but there is the trace of a smile on her face.

×

The hot summer days pass slowly. I no longer go to the jail, and I begin to find it difficult to think of myself as the executioner. Who am I? After considering this question, I come up with one answer: I am what I do. The problem is that now all I do is wait. In a way, I guess that is my duty. Yet I feel embarrassed by this idleness, especially when I reflect that I am still being paid. It occurs to me that I can make new duties for my position. That maybe there is some project I can help on, such as improving the grounds of the jail, or mending the wall near the stream in town. But I have few skills other than swinging an axe, and I do not know how the town manager would feel if I took on other kinds of work, or how other people in town would react.

I think about the word "inhumane." The government, after listening to the new thinking, decided executions might be inhumane. It is the first time I have heard this word. The meaning seems clear enough: something that is not human, something that goes against what it is to be human. But I cannot see anything more human than to provide a quick and clean way out of this life. If the government decides executions are now inhumane, why not other things too? Why not the way it fights the rebels, for example?

I forget these sorts of questions on my walks. Now that I have more time, I go farther and farther afield. In the west the nearest village, a sad little place where everyone raises cattle, is some twenty miles away. I remember it from my trips with my father. I never go that far, but I start to go past where the stream turns south. Beginning there, the wheat fields end and the ground becomes dry and sandy and only low shrubs grow, and it seems like I can see forever. I walk and walk.

At home I spend a lot of time lying in bed. Sometimes I stare at the pattern of cracks on the wall opposite the door, above the wooden table. If I look long enough, they form shapes from the world: trees or clouds or even faces. Sometimes I read from *Histories of the New World*. I water the garden every other day, and I buy a daily loaf of bread for Lena and me. Though there is not much I can do for her, I care for her as best I can. She is my wife and I owe her that.

Once a week, I visit Emmer in the early afternoon. This is something I look forward to, something that makes everything else easier. My second visit goes much the same as the first, except I do not encounter the jailer afterward. Even so, I tell Lena I drank with him and relate to her the gossip he supposedly shared, a story I make up about the grocer. He has been arrested, I say, for bringing supplies from the coast for the rebels. She smiles a little at this.

The third time I see Emmer, I decide to find out what exactly she will permit. I try everything I can think of, even the things Lena would not allow, and Emmer does what I want without protest, though she seems annoyed. I ask her what is wrong, but she will not tell me. At home I tell Lena more made-up gossip I claim I got while drinking with the jailer. This time it is a story I thought up about how one of the rebels was arrested in the brothel. I say the government is considering ending the stay to execute him.

On my fourth visit, Emmer is not in the room of women playing cards. I request to speak with her. The master of the house, Bersil, says this is not possible at the moment. I tell him I will wait, but he says she will not be available for at least a few days. A woman in the room laughs. I ask if something is wrong with Emmer. He says nothing is wrong and tells me to choose someone else. Maybe it is the time when she bleeds. Or maybe she left the brothel and returned to her homeland. I look at the other women. It is as if something rotten were in my stomach. I tell Bersil I will soon be back. At home, I explain to Lena that the jailer did not meet me as planned. I say he has fallen in love with a prostitute and that I am worried about him.

The next week is torture: I spend much of the time debating whether I should return to the brothel to see if Emmer is "available," to use the word of Bersil, the so-called master of the house. In the end I always decide to wait, to keep to my routine. If I go back and she is not there again, I will not know what to do.

I lie on the bed and stare at the wall opposite the door. The cracks shift and mix until they form her face. She looks at me with a serene expression.

After a week I return and she is there, in the room where the women play cards and chat. We go upstairs and I ask where she has been.

"Here," she replies. "Where else?"

"I came to see you. Did you go home?"

"This is my home. I must have been sick."

"You were sick?"

She laughs lightly. "You don't need to worry."

"It would be better if you came with me. My house is small, but there is enough room. You will not mind my wife." I realize as I say this that in fact I cannot bring her home, that there is not enough room, that she and Lena would not get along.

Emmer laughs again, showing me her two neat rows of teeth. "What would you do with me? You would soon grow bored, and so would I. Here at least I have my friends. It's better if you come to see me."

She caresses my thigh, and soon we are on the bed. Afterward she rises to open a window. Fresh hill air rushes into the room. In the distance I see the graveyard.

"Do you like it here?" I ask.

"It's not too bad." She lies next to me. "Sometimes the work is dull."

"With me?"

"No, not with you. You are very lively." She runs her hand down my chest and there is a moment of silence.

"Do you go to town sometimes?"

"Why would I go to town? The master of the house gives me what I need here, and in town the people act strangely. One time, when a girl went into town, a man became angry when she did not look the way he expected. He attacked her. Another man tried to kidnap a girl. There is nothing for me in town. Sometimes I go to the stream when I have a day off. Last winter I walked into the hills. It was pretty but I got cold after a while."

"You weren't scared of the rebels?"

"My brother was a rebel. If I told them, they would let me go."

"He's not a rebel anymore?"

"He was killed."

After a few moments, I ask, "How was he killed?"

"Fighting in the countryside."

I feel relief. I do not know how it would be between us if I executed him. But she does not seem very emotional about his death. "Do you support the rebels?"

"It doesn't matter. Everything will be the same, whoever wins."

I try to understand what she means. I do not know much about the rebels, or why they fight. I decide to change the subject. "How do you pass the time when you aren't working?"

"In the morning, we usually sit on the roof."

"What's on the roof?"

"There is just a view."

"Can I see?"

"You would have to entertain us."

"That's fine," I say. "I know many tricks." I rise naked from the bed and bend over into a handstand, careful not to knock into the wall or bed. I feel my privates flip down as I swing my feet up, and Emmer laughs. I hold the handstand for a few seconds.

"You have good balance," she says.

"You need good balance to be an executioner."

"That's not true!" She laughs again.

Soon my hour is up, and we go downstairs.

At home I tell Lena that, according to the jailer, the rebels kidnapped a woman who went walking in the hills. A party of soldiers has gone to search for her, I say, and the town is in a state of alarm, with a curfew in effect.

Over the following weeks, I give up my routine and visit Emmer as often as I want. Sometimes she is busy, and I wait for her. She only grows angry if I ask her to see no one but me. One day we spend five entire hours together. I am sure she likes me, but always I must pay, and always by the hour. Those are the rules.

Summer changes into fall. The leaves on the cottonwoods along the stream turn yellow and it becomes a little cool at night, while the winds die down. Outside town the fields are replanted with the winter wheat crop, and soon the new shoots poke up from the earth.

One day I check my hiding place in the wall and see that I do not have enough money to visit Emmer again. In fact, I barely have enough to continue buying food until I am paid in three weeks. I cannot remember when I counted my money last, but it is hard to believe that I spent almost all of my savings, and my salary. For a moment I wonder if Lena could have taken some. But no, she would not have had any chance to spend it. She only leaves her chair to use the toilet outside.

I am not sure what to do. There are not many ways for someone like me to make money.

The next morning the problem seems even more serious. It has been more than a day since I last saw Emmer, and I have gotten used to visiting her every afternoon. After debating whether to risk embarrassment, I decide to put my trust in her kindness. In the afternoon I walk to the brothel.

Bersil greets me warmly, as usual, and brings me to the room where the women sit and play cards. When I enter, Emmer rises and comes to me. I whisper to her that I do not have enough money. She looks at the master of the house. He has overheard.

"How will you pay?" he asks.

"I can pay after I get my salary."

He scratches at his beard. "I'm sorry, no credit."

I think for a moment. "I can work."

He smiles. "What will you do?"

I reach out and touch Emmer's waist. "But Emmer will allow it."

She does not answer, and he says, "It's not up to Emmer."

"Let him," she says. "You know he will pay."

"I have a little money," I say.

"How much?" he asks.

I tell him. He shakes his head.

"Let him," she says again. "Can't we ignore your rules for once?"

He turns toward her. "Why should I change the rules?" he says slowly. "These rules give you a place to sleep and food to eat. You forget yourself."

I glance at the other women. They look down at their feet and pretend not to pay attention, though the room is so small that I could cross it with five large steps. Emmer smiles at me, as if to say: *There is nothing I can do. He is the master of the house.* And maybe also: *It will be alright. Come back when you have enough money.* But I want to see her now. Must every moment of her time be accounted for? I imagine pushing Bersil aside and forcing my way upstairs with her. Maybe he would follow us, and I would turn on the stairway and, swatting away his arms, take his neck in my strong hands. He would beg for mercy, and I would let him go, and he would leave us alone.

Then I realize that the whole situation is my fault, that I must find a way to get more money. Bersil has always been kind to me. I mumble an apology and Emmer gives me a kiss goodbye. Bersil walks me to the entrance.

"Don't make it difficult for us," he says from the doorway. "We don't care about anything else, as long as you have money."

At home I do not tell any made-up gossip to Lena, though she looks at me when I enter. I lie on the bed and mull over my options.

After a while, I open *Histories of the New World.*

The section I read describes a people who would choose someone cruel and physically weak as their leader. They believed these qualities showed the favor of the gods: cruelty because it reflected the natural order, and weakness because only the weak saw the world as it was. Usually they chose men. After naming this person, they took away his possessions and renounced all affection for him. He then lived on charity.

Another of their customs was to appoint seven servants who had to obey the commands of everyone but the ruler. They considered this an honor and selected whoever had outdone others in the past year, such as through successful hunting or beautiful beadwork.

The book relates that, after leaving a fort in the interior, a foreigner wandered to the area and began living among them. He soon abused the servants. When they chose him as one, he refused to follow orders, and they cast him out. Two years later, he returned with an armed force and put to death all the men, having some buried alive. He took the women and children as slaves. Since then, he has become a colonial administrator.

Like other sections in the book, this one puzzles me. I don't see how, for example, cruelty reflects the "natural order." I guess this people saw the world as cruel, but such a view does not make much sense to me. Things like Lena's accident, or me not having enough money to see Emmer, might be called cruel. But others are clearly not, like my meeting Emmer or my still being paid at all. Also, a lot is neither cruel nor kind, like how the stream flows downhill and not up, or the fact that cottonwood leaves turn yellow in fall.

What I find myself returning to is how, among this people, the ruler is treated poorly, while the servants are honored even though they are insulted. This seemed so odd when I first read it that I wondered if the author of *Histories* made up some parts, just like I make up stories to tell Lena. I know this is what my father thought. But maybe the meaning is that anyone, even someone looked down on, can be a ruler. And if anyone can be a ruler, then anyone can be an executioner, then anyone can be anything.

In the morning, I fill two of Lena's baskets with basil and tarragon leaves from her garden. I am not sure how exactly to sell the herbs, but it cannot be that difficult. I make my way to the crossing, then past the inn to the market, to where Lena hurt herself.

I see the patchwork cloth roof from far away. It reminds me of old, wrinkled skin. As I approach, I smell the raw meat hanging from hooks at the nearby butcher houses and the overripe apricots piled neatly on a piece of cloth on the corner. There is also a trace of the stream on the other side of the market, a whiff of cool hill air and pine.

It is not busy. Market day is Saturday. I walk under the roof and between the wooden columns, passing sellers of beans and flour and almonds and apricots and pears and eggs. I can feel eyes on me. For all I know this is normal. For all I know everyone stares at you in the market. But nobody tries to sell me anything. Maybe they can see, from my baskets of herbs, that I have come to sell too.

I go to one of the empty wooden platforms on the far side of the market, near the walled stream. I arrange my baskets on either side and try to find a comfortable position in the center of the low platform. First I sit cross-legged, but that hurts my joints, and I turn my legs to one side. Then I lose feeling below my knees, so I sit on the edge, with my feet resting on the ground and a basket on either side of me. Because I am heavy, I must lean far back to prevent the platform from flipping over. Each time I move, the wood creaks.

The other sellers watch me from their platforms, as do the few people strolling among the narrow lanes. Soon a woman approaches from the other end of the market. She inspects the contents of my baskets, rummaging through them with her papery hands.

"You can't sell here," she says.

"Why? There is no one else here." A woman is selling red peppers at the platform across from mine, but the others nearby are empty.

"Reserved," she says, patting the thin strips of wood. "Someone has paid for the week." She is chewing on something, but I cannot see what.

"Whoever reserved it is not here," I say. "So why can't I use it?" I am tired of so many rules and restrictions. I only want to sell the herbs.

"Reserved," she repeats. "Come with me and I'll show you where you can sell." She leans to one side and spits out the shells of a seed. The ground is dotted with rubbish: pits and bits of rope and the shells she is chewing.

Gathering the baskets, I slide forward on the platform. The other end lifts into the air, and I hop off so as not to overturn it. I feel my face grow red. She laughs and leads me to the west side of the market, to a platform beside a garlic seller.

"Here," she says, and puts out her hand.

"Why are you putting out your hand?"

"You think you get to sell for free?"

It takes me a moment to realize what she means. "How much does it cost?" She tells me. It is not much. Still, I am not rich. "That is only for today?"

She nods and gives me the weekly price.

Beyond the rows of low platforms, I see a woman squatting on the ground in front of three baskets. "What if I go out there?" I ask, pointing.

She continues to look at me. "Go in the street if you like. That woman sells very little, and at a low price. People prefer to shop inside the market."

The woman seated behind mounds of garlic nods in agreement, and so I pay and sit carefully on the edge of the platform, a basket on either side of me.

Few shoppers stop to look at what I am selling. I wonder if I am frightening because of my size, or because I am a man. All the other sellers are women. I make an effort to smile so as to appear friendly, and I keep my eyes on the ground. Still, no one comes. After a while my mouth grows tired and I relax, but I have held it in the same position for so long that it feels as if I am still smiling.

By lunchtime, I grow worried I will sell nothing. The garlic seller has had many customers. She seems kind, and after she begins eating her lunch, I ask what her trick is.

"There's no trick," she says. She swallows a piece of bread and laughs pleasantly. Her food is hidden by the mounds of garlic around her. "These people come every other day, sometimes every day. They know us and we know them. Why are you selling here?"

"These are my wife's herbs. We do not need them."

She nods. "If you wait long enough, people will buy."

"Do you want to buy some?"

She laughs again. "Do you want to buy my garlic?"

She finishes eating and lies down on her platform to rest. I continue to sit. Other sellers lie down too and soon the market seems as if it is abandoned because only the piles or baskets of food are visible on the platforms. Occasionally a shopper wanders in from the street and stops at a platform and then that seller sits up.

More shoppers arrive and the market comes back to life. Instead of looking down at the ground, I follow the shoppers with my eyes as they move among the wooden columns, just like I was followed by eyes when I arrived. But it is not the same. I do not feel like a seller.

Having not thought to bring any lunch, I chew on a few basil leaves.

A woman approaches and asks me how much my tarragon costs. I am surprised by her question. For some reason I thought the price would be set already.

"How much will you give me?" I ask.

She picks up a handful and offers a small sum. Is that all tarragon is worth? I have never bought any before.

"How much for all of it?" I ask.

"I don't want all of it," she says.

I sell her the tarragon.

A boy approaches, dragging his mother behind him by the hand. "Aren't you the executioner?" he asks.

I notice the garlic seller peering at me. She must not have recognized me. Maybe she did not expect to see the executioner selling herbs. How many people saw me and knew who I was? How many did not? "Maybe I am," I tell him.

"What are you doing here?" His mother tries to shush him and pull him away, but only halfheartedly. She must also be curious.

"I'm selling herbs. What does it look like?"

"Are you going to execute someone?"

"Not now."

"Later?"

"Maybe not."

He is silent a moment. "How can you do the one thing, and then another?"

"It is hard," I confess.

He considers this and continues to stare at me. I stare back, but he does not seem to mind, so I turn toward his mother. She finally pulls him away.

I feel flustered after they leave, and I do not look around. I think of what the garlic seller said: *They know us and we know them.* Maybe that is the problem. The boy was not used to me, so he came and questioned me. I am not used to the market, so I have sold almost nothing. I must make new routines for myself.

"I thought Lena was married to a farmer," the garlic seller says.

I turn toward her. "How did you know Lena was my wife?"

"There are not many herb sellers." She smiles, pleased with herself.

I am silent for a while. "A farmer?"

"That is what she said."

I do not reply.

"But she never gave a name," she continues. "She never even said where she lived. When she had her accident, no one knew who to send word to."

So that is why nobody told me, why I had to wander into town at night to look for her when she did not return. "You were here when it happened?"

"Oh yes. She was right there." She gestures at another platform not far away. "That was hers. She stepped onto the edge to hang a basket from the column. But she fell back into a woman who was walking by, then rolled off and hit her head on the ground. Afterward she couldn't keep her balance. She kept leaning into things, and when we asked her what was wrong, she was silent, only looked at you with this strange face. We made her lie down and sent for the doctor."

This is the same story, more or less, that the doctor told me when I finally found her at his house, before he explained to me that she might not get better.

"I heard she lost the power of speech," the garlic seller says.

I do not reply right away. Then I ask, "What would she talk about at the market?"

"Gossip. She liked to gossip." She sells a few garlic bulbs to a woman who keeps her back to me. "She also talked about how, one of these days, she was going to buy a shop of her own. She chattered about that a lot." She chuckles. "She was always talking about her plans. She was one of those people. I didn't believe her. You could see she was only trying to impress you."

I nod.

"Has she gotten better?"

"She can say a few words."

"It must be hard to take care of her."

I say nothing.

"And then to be executioner, too. How do you do it?" She smiles and leans forward slightly.

I can see that she wants to hear about my life. My instinct is to please her, to tell her everything, but there is something that stops me. Like Lena she is a gossip. Whatever I say will make its way back to more sellers, and to others in town, and then maybe when I pass they will laugh.

Still, I cannot refuse her. She has treated me well. And so I decide to lie to her, to make up details about my life.

I am quiet for a while as I think. Then I tell her that, although the doctor said Lena will probably not get better, he gave me instructions for a special drink, and I make it for her daily. The drink is supposed to strengthen her mind, but the cost of the ingredients has drained our savings. That is why I have come to sell herbs.

I say I do exercises with her based on the doctor's directions, opening my mouth and moving my tongue in a certain way while she imitates me. In fact, I tried to do this for a while, figuring it would help, but after a short time she refused to continue.

I explain I also do exercises to maintain my fitness as executioner. The garlic seller makes a little sound of encouragement at this point, and I can see she is committing everything to memory. I tell her I take my axe and practice driving it into a wooden block, that I lift it over my head again and again, that I go for long walks to help my circulation. I say that when I return home, I douse a cloth in warm water and give it to Lena, and she puts it on her neck. Actually, she used to be fond of doing this, but she has not bothered since she became sick.

The garlic seller hangs on to every word, and I enjoy lying to her. I enjoy making up a new life for myself. But then I wonder if I should do all the things I describe.

As the sunlight fades, she begins to put the garlic bulbs she has arranged on the platform into baskets. The other sellers also start to pack up their wares. I have nothing to pack up, and so I take one of my baskets in each hand and rise. The garlic seller asks if I will return tomorrow and I tell her yes. But I am not sure my trip to the market has been worth it. I can only buy a few loafs of bread with what I earned. I am not much closer to paying for a visit to Emmer.

Lena told others that I was a farmer. I realized long ago that she disliked my position, but for her to be so ashamed as to lie about it seems like something else entirely.

When I pass the two windows, I do not look inside. At the door I see her sitting on her chair, staring out the one window as usual. I place the baskets of herbs under the porch, not far from my axe, and I put a fresh loaf under the bowl on the table. I lay down on the bed. The temperature has dropped, so I pull the blanket over my body. I should close the windows, give Lena a blanket of her own. I should also slice bread for us to eat. But I am tired of helping her, and I am not hungry. I want to rest for a few minutes. Anyway, she can always do something for herself.

×

I wake in the dark with moonlight streaming through the windows. It is chillier than before, and I rise and fasten the windows' oak panels. Although air leaks in around the edges, the wood will keep out some of the chill.

Lena is in her chair.

"Why don't you come to bed?" I say in the dark.

Her head slumps to the side. She is asleep. I lift her up and lay her down on the bed. From the chest in the corner I remove the second blanket and drape it over her. I lie down beside her. It takes me a while to fall back asleep. The closed windows are two square outlines of light against the wall, and even when I shut my eyes, I can see them.

×

In the morning, Lena's blanket lies on the floor. She must have tossed and turned during the night, though she did not wake me. I rise and open the windows. The sun hides behind the hills on the other side of town. It is cool, cooler than usual for this time of year.

I spread the blanket over Lena again and sit down at the table. Then I take the loaf and cut myself two thick slices. I eat them slowly. The bread does not taste like anything. At the well I raise a pail of water and drink, then pour the rest into the jug.

After I use the toilet, I see that Lena has woken and moved to her chair. I pour some water into a cup and hand it to her. I cut another slice of bread and give that to her too.

"Maybe you are ashamed of me," I say, taking a seat at the table. She continues to look out the window while eating her bread. She breaks off lumps and forms them into balls before putting them in her mouth. "I don't think that matters now. And I don't think it matters that you did not like to listen to me. And I don't think it matters that, as time went on, you treated me like I was stupid."

She turns toward me, her face blank.

"I'm sleeping with another woman," I say. "She does not care what my job is."

She continues to look at me, chewing slowly. "Always," she says, her mouth full.

"No, just recently."

She brushes at the air with her hand. "Always. Always." She begins choking. I walk around her and push her forward a little, then hit her softly on her back until she spits up a spongy piece of bread. I pick it off the ground and throw it out the window. Then I wipe my hand on my pant leg.

What does she mean? I go back to my seat. She has turned away from me. *Always*. Then I understand: *Always*, or, *Go ahead. What do I care?*

I begin to regret saying anything. She is sick, and I should not be angry with her. I consider apologizing, but maybe there is no point. What I said will always be between us.

Outside the two baskets of herbs rest on the ground beside the wall, the green leaves still unwilted. I could bring them again to the market, but how do I know I will sell more than yesterday? How long will it take for people to grow used to an executioner selling herbs? Then there is the garlic seller. She will no doubt have more questions, and I do not want to answer them. I am tired of being treated as an oddity.

From the edge of the garden I watch the sun rise. I return inside and lie on the bed. Eventually I decide to take a walk. Instead of heading west, I go into town, at first I am not sure why. I follow the road to the crossing, then pass the baker's, breathing in the smell of fresh bread. Nearby a boy kicks a ball against the side of a house. At the new bridge I follow the stream east, and soon the walls on either side end and I stand near the reeds looking up the grassy slope at the brothel. It seems like a fortress, though from my position I can see the pergola on the roof. I walk up the slope and stand against the south wall. Voices drift down to me, female voices mixed with each other, distant and peaceful. They make me think of afternoons in bed with Emmer, of her perfume, a smell somewhere between lavender and pine, of the loose flesh at her waist, of her hair falling against my skin. For hours I stand there, in the sun, my back to the wall, listening. Finally I hear things knocking into each other and the voices disappear. I wait for a while to see if they will return. When they do not, I walk home.

That night it becomes clear Lena is sick. Her skin is hot to the touch and her eyes seem to have sunk deeper into her skull. When I ask her what is wrong, she only shakes her head or says her own name. She will not accept any of the food I offer. If I put bread in her mouth, she spits it out. I help her to the toilet. Then I bring her to bed and wrap her in both our blankets. Though the cool spell has passed, I want to keep her as warm as possible. In the middle of the night I wake up feeling a little chilly, and I get under the blankets with her.

The next morning she is coated in sweat and seems worse. I give her water but still she will not take food. Rather than bring her to the chair, I leave her in bed.

At the table, I debate whether to fetch the doctor. I will not be paid for two more weeks. To judge by the last time he saw her, after she fell at the market, a visit will cost all the money we have left. Then we will not have enough for food. It seems best to wait another day to see if she improves.

I stare out the window. In the back of my mind, I hear the voices from the brothel roof, like a steady soft chiming. I look at Lena. At the moment there is nothing I can do other than wait to see if she gets better. I will just take a short walk.

Crossing the town, I return to the same spot against the brothel's south wall. I press my back against the rough stucco and listen to the haze of voices floating down from the roof. I close my eyes. After a while my body grows warm and light-feeling.

Then one of the voices becomes louder. It is of medium pitch and slightly raspy. I make out words, complete sentences. The voice is talking about a man, about how he does not seem to want to sleep with her. I hear, “Hey, what are you doing?” There is a short pause. Then: “Look, it’s the executioner!”

I look upward but remain against the wall, so that the back of my head presses against the small knobs of the stucco. A woman’s face balances on the border between the white wall and bright blue sky. Soon it is joined by others. Among the newcomers I make out Emmer.

“What are you doing there?” she asks.

I take a few steps forward and turn so I do not have to look directly up. I am not sure what to say. “I was just listening.” And then, because this does not seem like enough of an explanation: “To your voices.”

“You were spying?” asks the raspy one.

“No, I could not hear what you said. Not until you came to the edge. I only listened to the sound.”

“Why would you do that?” asks another voice.

There is a silence. “I am not sure,” I confess. “There is something about it.”

They talk among themselves, and then Emmer asks, “Why haven’t you come to see me?”

“I am waiting to be paid. I have no money. I tried to see you, remember, but Bersil said I needed money.”

“This is a brothel, not a charity,” the raspy one says, and the others laugh, including Emmer.

Then Emmer says to the others, “Why not let him up here?

He has come all this way, and I'm tired of listening to your stories."

"But he's the executioner!" one says.

"And what are you?" Emmer replies.

They argue among themselves, and then a rope falls against the wall, just missing me. I turn toward a nearby window, worried that the master of the house or someone else might look out and see me, but the slats remain closed.

"Can you climb?" Emmer asks.

I nod. The rope is thin and dried out and I am afraid it will snap, but I pull myself up, hand over hand over hand, while I walk up the wall. When I look up I see a row of faces watching me intently. By the time I reach the top they have moved back, and I swing one leg over. I grasp the edge of the wall, first with one hand, then with the other, and awkwardly roll onto the roof.

"You're strong," one says, and I feel myself blush.

Altogether there are eight women in pajamas. Some have shawls wrapped around their shoulders. I recognize all eight, though they look a little different in the sunlight. Behind them pillows and a hammock lie in the shade of the cloth-covered wooden pergola. The rope I have climbed is tied to a column with a basket of clothes at its base.

"Let's get out of the sun," Emmer says, and gestures for me to follow her. I pull the rope up, and Emmer and I sit together on the large hammock. There are not enough pillows for everyone, and another woman joins us so that I am sitting between her and Emmer.

"You can only stay for a short while," says the raspy one. She sits cross-legged on a pillow.

"What's your name?" I ask her.

"My name?" She laughs. "You can call me L."

"She's in a bad mood," says the woman sitting with Emmer and me. "Yesterday her brother said he would no longer allow her in his house." She adds, "I'm Jana." I realize she is the one who plays the game with the jailer.

"Why tell him that?" snaps L. "At least I have a brother. You came here on your own."

"Isn't that better than being sent—"

"My wife is sick," I say, to join the conversation.

L turns to me. "Then why aren't you with her?"

I feel my face redden again. I almost answer, *I could not help coming here*, but then the others ask what is wrong with her. I tell them she came down with a fever overnight. I leave out that I did not wrap her in a blanket before I fell asleep. Surely she could have gotten a blanket herself if she was cold. The women suggest different treatments. One says to let her feet sit in hot water, another to feed her plenty of onions. Emmer is silent. Her thigh rests against my chest because of her position higher up on the hammock.

"But your wife was already sick," she says, and everyone grows quiet to listen. I can see she is respected. "She fell in the market and stopped speaking. All you do is take care of her, and what has she ever done except make you feel bad about yourself?"

The harshness of her words changes the mood. I cannot decide whether I should try to defend Lena, and so I say nothing. Emmer does not know everything, does not understand me as well as she thinks. She is not aware, for example, that it was probably my carelessness that led to Lena's fever. She does not seem to see that, without Lena, I will be more alone than I am now. I will only have her, Emmer, who I must pay to see, and an uncertain future as an executioner. I know she wants what is best for me, that she thinks Lena is a burden. And maybe she is partly right. But I still have my duty to her. I am still her husband.

The silence lengthens. Emmer says, "Why don't you show us your trick," and I take her proposal as a peace offering, as an attempt to erase, or at least cover up, what she said before.

I rise and, in the sunlight outside the pergola, swing myself into a handstand, holding it for five or so seconds.

There is scattered applause, and I return to my feet. Unsteadily I make my way back to the hammock and sink into its net. Emmer rests her hand on my neck for a moment.

After a silence, L describes her relationship with a customer, starting where she seems to have left off. With the others I listen. From certain details, such as that he always wears platform shoes, and has short hair in front and a long sheet of hair in back that he combs carefully, I guess she is talking about the town manager. Often, she says, he speaks about the history of the town, or the Republic, and how he rose to his position. He works himself into such a state, she explains, that they rarely sleep together. Instead, he lectures her while he paces the room or absentmindedly toys with his buttons. She is the only person he can speak freely to, he says. If she makes an advance, he ignores it, and if they manage to get into bed, sometimes he recounts his professional grudges in the act. This is the word L uses: *act*. Everything he says comes down to one thing, she explains: that he is dissatisfied with his position, that he thinks he should be province manager or have an even higher title. You might think she should be glad he is not interested in the act, because his breath is foul, and anyway he is not attractive. But in fact she has come to dread his visits, because he makes her doubt her own charms. He makes her feel worthless.

The story is greeted by some chuckles and, at the end, shows of sympathy. A round-faced woman begins speaking, and it seems as if she is afraid her story will not be appreciated. She starts by saying she wants to leave the brothel but has not saved enough money. Then she tells of a man who offered to marry her. At this point L interrupts and asks who she means. When she names him, L hisses and says he is a reptile and once proposed to her as well. No man will marry a whore, she adds.

"That's not true," I say. "I would, only I am married already."

My words are met with general laughter. Sensing that I have said something foolish, I laugh too. My chortles come easily, grow louder and louder, and it feels as if my chest and then my entire body were expanding. It is the first time I have laughed in a while. Once more Emmer places her hand on my neck. When I look up at her, she smiles.

The women continue to talk about the brothel's customers while a breeze comes off the hills. When the conversation fades, Jana asks if I will rub her back. I turn and take her shoulders in my hands and knead them softly. Even though I am sitting between Emmer and Jana, with Emmer's thighs and hand resting on me, and Jana's delicate shoulder blades under my hands, I have not been thinking of the act, to use L's word. At first, it's true, I was excited by the way the thin pajamas clung to the women's skin in the breeze, but at some point I stopped noticing their bodies.

The quiet is interrupted by a shout from the stairway on the north side of the roof. The women slowly rise from their seats, taking the cushions and piling them in a small shed. Emmer gestures for me to climb down.

"What's happening?" I ask her.

"That was Bersil. It's time for us to go."

Reluctantly I throw the rope over the wall, and Jana waves goodbye as I go over the edge. When I reach the ground, I look up and see the thin cord disappearing into the sky.

On the way home, I remember Lena, feverish and alone. I walk faster. I find her lying in bed just as I left her, her skin maybe hotter than before and still covered in sweat. She will not eat any food, not bread or pieces of tomato. Whatever I put in her mouth remains there unchewed. Carefully I pour water down her throat. Remembering the advice I was given, I heat a pail of water over the stove outside. I try to force her to sit up on the bed and put her feet in the pail, but she keeps falling back.

Her sickness is serious, I realize, and so I go for the doctor, but when I get to his house on the other side of the stream, his servant tells me he has been called to a village north of town. I ask if he will be back by tomorrow. She says she is not sure and shuts the door.

There are only a few hours of daylight left by the time I return home. I cut myself three thick slices of bread and dip them in oil. Lena will still not take food, and when I accidentally pour too much water in her mouth, she gags.

I lie in bed beside her. I try to read *Histories of the New World*, but the words pass through my mind without leaving any trace, like wind through a wheat field. The heat radiates from her body and makes me uncomfortable.

In the morning her condition has worsened, and I set out right away for the doctor's house. The sun is just visible above the line of the hills when I arrive. I knock until the servant answers the door, her hair down.

"I'm sorry," I say. "But I've come for the doctor. My wife—"

She shuts the door in my face with a thwack. After a while the door opens and the doctor looks at me from under his thick eyebrows.

"You? I told you there's nothing I can do for her."

"No, it's not that. She has a fever."

"A fever," he says.

"She sweats all the time, and she won't eat. And her body is stiff."

"I see. You have money?"

"Yes."

"How much?"

"Enough."

"How much?"

I tell him.

"That's all?"

"That's what you charged before."

"Alright. Wait here a moment. Wait right here."

He shuts the door and reappears after what seems a half hour, having changed out of his robe. Instead of taking the main road we cut through the narrow alleys behind the inn. At one point he stops to chat with someone he knows, and I wait for him. When he stops again I cannot control myself.

"Doctor, we must hurry," I say, interrupting his conversation with a woman at her doorstep. He looks at me with his eyebrows raised, the skin on his forehead bunched together. He says goodbye to her. Afterward he makes a point of walking even faster than me.

Finally we reach my house. The doctor peers in.

"Dirty in here, isn't it. Can you bring her outside?"

"But there is nowhere to put her."

He continues to eye the room from the doorway. I follow his gaze. The house is not dirty.

"Please," I say.

The doctor sighs and enters. From his bag he takes a series of instruments. He forces a long piece of metal into Lena's throat, prods and touches her, looks closely at her eyes and ears.

"Has she been moving about? Traveled anywhere?" he asks without turning around.

"No."

"Defecated recently?"

"What?"

"Emptied her bowels."

"Not for a few days. At least, not that I know of."

"That you know of?"

"Sometimes I take walks and I'm gone for a few hours."

He turns and scowls at me, as if this is a crime. "Has she been eating?"

"Not these last few days."

"And before then?"

"She ate, yes, but not much."

"She has grown very thin since I saw her last. Very thin."

He asks more questions. While he is thorough, the way he handles Lena makes her seem like an animal.

Before long he packs up his things. Lena lies on the bed, her face waxy, her blankets tossed aside.

"How is she?" I ask.

He remains silent for a while. Then, rising from the bed with his bag in one hand, he turns to me. "I'm sorry to have to tell you this, but I would be surprised if she recovered."

"You mean she might—"

"I'm afraid so."

"Why?"

"A new sickness. Before now I've only seen it in the countryside. The very strong recover."

We both look at her. She seems anything but strong. Her neck is pitifully thin, her arms have no flesh, and I can see her veins through her forehead.

"Look at it this way," he adds. "She was not leading a particularly rich life."

"Can I do anything?" I ask.

"Make sure she has plenty of fresh air. Feed her hot water. Soup if she can stomach it. That's all you can do." He surveys the house. "You might give this place a good cleaning. Oh, and monitor yourself for symptoms. Chest pain, vertigo, fatigue."

"Is it my fault?"

He looks around the house again, shaking his head. "How would I know whose fault it is? People die all the time. Often it makes no sense to look for fault."

He puts his hand out and I take the money from my pocket and give it to him.

"Thank you, doctor," I say, but he has already hurried out the door. I glimpse his broad hat through the windows.

I cover her with blankets again, wiping the sweat from her brow. Her eyes flicker open and there is a look of terror on her face. Maybe she heard the doctor's prediction. But no, her eyes are unfocused. She must be seeing something with her mind's eye. Her pale lips move, but no sound comes out. Then I hear her say her own name. Again and again she repeats it, her voice growing louder and louder until she abruptly hushes.

Despite the doctor's words, I cannot help thinking it is my fault she has a fever, that it is because I did not care for her properly. Something else he said bothers me: *She was not leading a particularly rich life.* He seemed to be saying that, for this reason, her death matters less. But why should the richness of her life make any difference? It is still a life.

I shuffle outside and heat water, then wait for it to cool a little so Lena will be able to drink it. I sit her up in bed, bending her body forward with difficulty, and press a cup to her lips. When I pour too fast, her mouth fills and water runs out over her chin, dripping onto the blankets. When the cup is nearly empty she begins coughing and spits up some of the water. I wipe her face and neck and wait for the fit to pass. Then I lie her down again. The blankets are damp in places, but they are the only ones we have.

Maybe the doctor is wrong and she will recover. Events are not so easy to predict. Who could have guessed that I would be caring for Lena, as I am now? And who could have guessed that Parliament would enact a stay?

A crunching at the doorway draws me out of my thoughts. I turn and see the jailer's boy.

"How long have you been there?" I ask from my seat on the bed.

"Not long," he says. His hands are clasped together. When he opens them I see his toy. He flicks it toward me, but I am in no mood for games. I feel as if he has trespassed, as if he is taunting me with his presence, and I hit the toy out of the air with the back of my hand, so that the two wooden discs fly apart and roll against the chest in the corner. He steps inside to collect them.

"What do you want?" I ask.

He returns to the doorway and keeps his face turned down as he puts the toy back together.

"My father sent me," he says, still looking down. "He says the town manager wants to see you. He says it's important. He says there is to be an execution."

"An execution?" My heart thuds against my chest. "Has the government ended the stay?"

He looks up and shrugs.

I turn away from him. An execution can only mean one thing: everything is as before. How long has it been? Maybe three months, though it seems longer.

Turning back, I notice he has a bruise on his left cheekbone, a purple blotch that fades into yellow around the edges.

"Your face," I say.

"Fighting," he says. There is silence for a while. Then he dips his head toward Lena. "What's wrong with her?"

"She's sick." I do not want to explain, but I know if he asks for more information, I will tell him exactly what the doctor said. But he does not ask. He only nods knowingly. "Is that all?"

"I refused to tell the other boys where you live." He puts the loop of string on his finger and I see him bring back his hand, but then he stops himself and clasps the toy between his palms.

"What boys?" Then I realize who he means.

"The boys who swore to hurt you."

"I didn't ask you to do that." I know I must care for Lena, that I must go see the town manager. What he is saying seems unimportant. "What do you want?" But he turns from the doorway without another word. Through the windows I see him pass.

I heat more water for Lena to drink, then decide she has had enough. Now that I am alone with her, I think of the boy and his bruise. Maybe he has been trying to win my goodwill all along. Maybe, as the jailer's son, he is treated like me: ignored, frowned at, talked down to. If so, I guess I owe him some sort of friendship. Some kindness.

I start for the town hall. A strong wind blows from the west, flattening the wheat fields on the edge of town. In the reception room on the fourth floor, the stone sculptures over the doorways, the large painting of men in brightly-colored robes and the patterned wood on the floor all seem less impressive. The town manager does not keep me waiting long.

"Excellent news," he says, rushing toward me from the doorway to his office. I remember what L said, how he visits her only so she can listen to him. He moves close enough that his rank breath fills my nostrils. "Still capable of performing your duties, I expect?"

"My wife is very sick."

"Excellent! What's that?" He squints as if standing in bright sunlight. "Well—she'll get better, no doubt. Do you need anything? Good."

"Could I have some of my salary before next week? You see, I had to pay the doctor."

"Yes, done, right away. Anything else?" When I shake my head, he strides to his office, leans inside and shouts: "Please compose a memorandum instructing the clerk to pay the executioner one half of his next month's salary." He moves back toward me, his shoes tapping on the wood.

"This town," he begins, "has a history of being overlooked. *Historia*. To inquire. To know. What I'm saying, I suppose, is that we must know this town by its history, as we must know each other by our histories. Isn't that right?"

I nod. I think for a moment of my book. It occurs to me that the town manager may have read it as well. But I doubt he would be willing to discuss it with me.

"During the old regime, the emperor stopped here on his tour of the outlying provinces," he continues. "But that was forty years ago—before your time, while I was just a boy. A population of five thousand may be small compared to the towns and cities of the north, but there is our strategic location to consider—our position at the heart of the rebellion, admittedly not a serious threat—it is this that puts us in the first rank of importance. And yet, we have been neglected. Even our representative ignores us, drinking and philandering in the capital. He claims he is overworked because he serves two large provinces, though they are only large geographically, not in population. He claims he has insufficient time to be always visiting. But I know what he does with his time."

He moves away from me, pacing the room.

"Now is my time to prove myself, now is *our* time." He claps his hands together and looks at me. "I will tell you why. The majority leader is visiting tomorrow as part of a personal tour of areas affected by the rebellion. He will be accompanied by certain prominent persons, and he has asked us for a small favor—an execution." He stops and looks at me, smiling in a childish manner, simply and affectionately.

"Does this mean Parliament has ended the stay?"

"No. The stay is still in effect. This is a favor."

I wait for him to go on.

"And a favor is like money. It can be exchanged for something else."

"Why does he—"

"The majority leader was against the stay, but the personages with him were among the supporters. He has convinced these personages to observe an execution—he wants to show them a clean and efficient execution—because in fact they have never seen one! And so he has asked me to arrange one. He considers it unlikely, as do I, that word will reach the capital, as remote as we are, and even if it does, he can excuse it on special administrative grounds. I have assured him you are a first-rate executioner. If you perform well, we may convince these personages that executions should continue. The stay may be annulled."

He speaks so quickly that it is difficult to understand everything. I go over his words in my head. He stops pacing and waits for a response.

"Will I get in trouble for disobeying Parliament?" I ask.

He sucks his smile into his face and waves his right hand. "What an idea! All responsibility falls on me. You are merely carrying out my orders. *Exequi*, to follow up, to pursue, to do—you, you see, are the doer." He laughs. "But why even think of this? This is the majority leader! He practically is the government."

I nod so he will stop staring at me. It is odd to be told to disobey the government, or part of the government. But I understand that, by showing the visitors a proper execution, I might help end the stay.

"I visited the jail this morning," he says. "They have stopped bringing in prisoners. There are only two left. One is very sick, I'm not sure what's wrong with him, and the other is missing an ear. For so distinguished an audience, it would be a shame to execute a sick man—it would be like serving old meat to an important guest. We must have someone still vigorous, missing ear or not."

I nod. I want to return home to check on Lena now that I have learned the news.

"I can see you're anxious to prepare," he says. "One last thing. To make the execution more ceremonious, I have supplied a wagon. It's at the jail. That way you can ride rather than walk to the square. How does that sound?"

I nod again.

"A final note. They are scheduled to depart at sunrise two

mornings from now. Let's have the execution after the midday rest tomorrow, but well before dinner. That way we'll minimize any effects on their digestion—they are from the capital, you know. Let's say two o'clock. I'll have the jailer send his boy for you. Is there anything you need?"

"My pay, please."

"Ah, yes." He disappears into his office and comes back with a signed slip of paper. "Take this to the clerk. Let me know if you want anything else. Remember, we are giving a performance tomorrow, eh. Let's do our best, isn't that right?"

Again I nod. Before I can leave he clutches my arm with his soft fingers.

"I know you will do well," he says.

He lets his hand slide off and I go downstairs to collect half my monthly salary. On my way home I stop at the baker's shop on the west side of town. Then I remember what the doctor said, and I make my way to the market to buy a chicken for soup. The stall I visit, along a side street, smells faintly of rot. The butcher is careful not to touch me when he takes my money and passes me the still-warm carcass of the chicken, gutted and plucked and wrapped in a sheet of rough brown paper.

At home Lena is the same. I boil a pot of water on the stove outside and drop in the chicken. I add sliced tomatoes and onions and a handful of basil and tarragon from the garden, like I remember her doing.

As I sit at the table to let the chicken cook, I close my eyes. After a while I see myself at the northwest corner of the square, axe in hand, while a prisoner kneels at the block of wood on the platform, his face hidden from me. On the west side of the square a large audience has gathered, and I recognize people from the market. Though I am the executioner, I am also part of the audience, and I watch myself as I cross the square and walk up the stairs to the platform. When I reach the top, I appear back on the ground and climb once more. Again and again I go up the stairs only to appear at the bottom. The crowd and also the prisoner wait for me in silence.

When the water starts to boil, I open my eyes. I remove some of the wood and stir the pot. The sun sinks into the wheat fields to the west. Though my eyes are open, I still see myself climbing the steps to the platform. Then the vision fades.

With the fork, I lift the chicken. It is odd that this jumble of flesh and bone smells pleasant. I tear off a morsel with my fingers and put it into my mouth. It is slippery against my tongue. Spitting it onto my palm, I see traces of pink, so I toss it down the slope to the east and lower the chicken back into the bubbling water.

After the chicken is completely cooked, I feed Lena a bowl of the broth, and though she does not look any better, she keeps it all down. I drink two bowls myself and eat a few pieces of the meat and a slice of bread. Then I put out the fire, leaving the pot covered on the stove. I drag the chest out from the corner and set a chair beside it. I bring my whetstone and axe inside.

What if the extremists are right, and an axe is not in keeping with the spirit of the times? Mine belonged to my father's father, the first executioner for the province. It is simple, that is true: a straight haft of ash, about five feet long, fitted into a single-bladed metal head. I have always thought there was beauty in its simple form, in the way a bowl or a door can be beautiful. Other tools might have its power, but not its uncomplicated grace. A rope, for example, is formed from many strands, and becomes tangled, and the threads or fibers soon stick out. A musket, with its many parts, is about as clumsy an object as I can think of.

I start to sharpen my axe, as I always do before an execution, but the scrape of stone against metal seems out of place in the twilight, with Lena wrapped in blankets on the bed. I will wait until morning.

×

When I open my eyes, it is dark, and terror paralyzes my body. The terror has no cause that I understand. My mind, while racing, is blank. Eventually the feeling dwindles and my muscles relax. After I shift onto my side, I fall back asleep.

When I wake again, it is still dark. I remain on the bed, motionless, until I realize it is too quiet. I stare at the blankets covering Lena. Tossing the blankets aside, I put my head to her breast. Her heart is still. "Lena," I say, but before I utter her name I understand that she will not answer. For a moment, it is as if someone were driving their hands into my chest. I recall the morning when my father died, leaving me alone for the first time. The sadness of this memory mixes with the grief I feel because Lena is gone. Then there is the knowledge that I have failed her, that I could have done more.

Gradually sunlight fills the house, and a pigeon enters through one of the windows and flies in a circle. It leaves through the same window. When I finally lift my head from Lena's breast, I see my axe and the whetstone. The sharp edge of the blade glints in the sunlight. I would prefer not to leave Lena's body on the bed while I carry out an execution. I would prefer to bury her beforehand.

Outside a breeze comes from the west. There is no room for Lena beside my father's grave, among the rock outcroppings behind the house. Across town I can see the graveyard in the blue shadow of the hills. I could fetch a cart from the jail and bring her there. But why should she be buried with people from town? No one there took any interest in her, or helped tend to her.

The rows of tarragon and basil sway in the light wind. Of course, I think: what better place? The garden was what she cared about most.

I stare at the dusty earth beneath the herbs. Then I tell myself I do not have much time. I take a shovel from the side of the house and go to the north end of the garden, where a patch of dirt separates the plants from the slope descending to the neighboring wheat field. When I thrust the point of the shovel into the ground, it barely breaks the surface. The sun has baked the dirt into a hard crust. I try again with the same result. Then I swing the side of the shovel's blade into the ground. When I realize what I am doing, I go inside for the axe. I return and use the blade to break up the topsoil. The earth underneath is dark and loose, and when I take up the shovel again I make rapid headway. Though my shoulders and arms begin to ache, I do not stop to rest.

Soon the ground is at the level of my shoulders, and I climb out. The hole is oval rather than rectangular, but seems big enough. I crouch and rest, panting.

Lena's body has started to grow rigid. I wrap her in one of the blankets, leaving her head uncovered and forcing her left arm against her side. Then I carry her to the grave. As I try to figure out how best to lower her, I see that the hole is too short. She needs another foot or so. I place her on the ground, on the side opposite the mound of dirt. But I do not like how she looks there, and I carry her back inside and lay her on the bed. I keep digging.

When I bring her out again, I set her down and jump into the hole, then carefully lower her and climb out.

Being wrapped in a blanket makes her head look very small, like maybe it is someone else's head, and for a moment I imagine she is another person. Then I look at her features. I say her name from my position at the edge of the grave.

Though I have seen many corpses, it has been a long time since I felt sick from looking at one.

When I buried my father, I said a few words about his life. The priest praises the dead for a fee, but he is lazy and hardly respected. Before he stopped attending executions, he made me uneasy with his jokes and the offhand way he treated the prisoners. Partly because of how he acts, I have trouble believing in the life he says follows death, or in the god he claims loves all people. But it is also because my father thought these things were lies.

Lena had no interest in the church. As I stand over her grave, I reflect on our many days together. I prefer to be truthful. I say, "I do not think I loved you, Lena, but we shared part of our lives. And I will miss you."

I try to summon a memory of her, something that will suit the moment. What comes to mind is an image of her at the table with her head thrown back in laughter. My limbs tremble, and a few tears inch down my cheeks.

I stare down at her. Then I begin filling the hole. The first shovelfuls hit her body with an unpleasant thump, but soon there is only the swish of dirt on dirt.

After I finish, I go to the well and drink deeply, pouring what is left of the pail over my head and washing my hands. I go inside and sit at the table. Though I'm not hungry, I force myself to eat a slice of the leftover loaf. Outside I fetch the axe, then wipe off the dirt and begin sharpening the blade.

Soon the jailer's boy appears on the road. He is without his toy.

"Why are you so dirty?" he asks.

Looking down, I see that my clothes are smeared with earth. "Lena is dead," I say.

He peeks inside the house. He avoids my eyes. He does not know how to respond. "Where?"

"I buried her."

A silence. "Sorry," he mumbles. Then, more loudly, "Hurry up, there's to be an execution."

"Let me rest for a moment," I say. I know I have no choice but to go.

"We don't have time. There are important people waiting."

I remain seated in silence while he fidgets, I am not sure for how long. Then I set the head of the axe on my shoulder. I walk more slowly than usual, and he has no trouble keeping up. A soreness pulses in my shoulders and back, but my damp hair feels good in the sun and I am thankful for the easy downward slope of the road to the jail. There seems to be a sweet smell in the air. I realize it is only the freshly dug earth clinging to my clothes. We walk in silence, and I try not to think of Lena.

At the jail entrance a soldier I do not recognize stands by a one-horse wagon. Flying from a pole at its front is the Republic's flag, its sky blue split lengthwise by a straight white line. The soldier says something I do not hear. I walk into the jail's courtyard and, after a moment, go to the cells.

Ear, standing in the shade, in the corner farthest from his cellmate, stares at my axe. Two sits on the ground. He has gotten worse. His swollen eyelids look like grapes that might burst if you touch them, and there is only a sliver of eyeball visible at the bottom edges. On his cheeks pus from his eyes has dried. Flies buzz around his head, and around the foul-smelling pail used as a toilet, and from time to time Ear swats furiously at them.

"It's these flies," he says. "These flies allow me no sleep." He smiles weakly. Behind me I hear the boy run into the house. "What are you doing with that?" Ear asks. "They have stopped the executions, remember?"

"The town manager has given me an order."

"Order? Ah, I see." He looks at Two. "Well, he is very sick. It's a shame, but he will probably not live in any case."

I realize what he means, but I only ask, "Do you know what's wrong with him?"

"His eyes—do you see his eyes?"

"Is that all?"

"He's unwell. Look at him."

"He might get better."

"How can he get better?" He gestures around him at the jail.

"You are to be executed," I tell him.

He does not understand me right away. Then he rushes to the front of the cell and grips the bars. "Me? Why me? Look at him—he will not live long. What sense does it make to execute me and not him?"

What sense does it make? I try to remember. The town manager said something about giving a better show. Though I do not see how it matters which of the prisoners is executed—a head will be chopped off, and that is show enough—that does not mean I can disobey.

Also, something in Ear's words bothers me. Two is sick, so he should be executed, he is saying. But Lena was sick, too. Sickness does not mean we give up on a person. I shake my head.

"He's sick!" he shouts.

"He might get better," I say again.

Keys jangle behind me. I turn and see the boy and his father.

"What happened to you?" the jailer asks.

"What do you mean?"

He gestures at my clothes.

"Lena died," I say, softly.

"What?"

The boy whispers to him, and the jailer looks at me strangely, as if I have done something wrong. "I'm sorry," he says to me. Then he goes to unlock the cell door. When Ear retreats to the back corner, the jailer moves inside and strikes him with a wooden baton that he carries on his belt. I hear the crack of a rib. He strikes him again and moves back, but Ear remains in the corner, clutching his side.

"Take him," Ear moans, gesturing to Two, who sits on the ground looking at the jailer from under his swollen eyelids.

The jailer advances again and continues to beat Ear. The baton makes a loud slapping sound on his skin, and now Ear is silent. Slap, I hear. Slap. Slap. *Slap.*

"Do I care if you are hungry?" the jailer asks as he hits him. "Do I care if there are too many flies?"

He is going too far. *Slap.* This is not what a jailer should do. *Slap.* I step into the cell and push him gently against the bars, pinning his arm and the baton against his side. I am much larger and it should take little effort, but my muscles, sore from digging the grave, ache with each movement.

"It will be painless," I say to Ear. "Come on."

It takes him a few moments to understand what I mean. Then he leaves the cell and I bring him to the wagon. I help him climb in. His skin is bruised and in some places cut, and he clutches his side, moaning softly.

Turning back, I see the jailer staring at me with hatred.

"Big to-do, isn't it?" asks the soldier.

I look at him. He must have seen the beating from the jail entrance. "What do you mean?"

"All this," he says, and grips the flagpole sticking up from the wagon.

We start our march to the square, the soldier leading the horse. The rumble and creak of the wheels mixes with the prisoner's moans. The noise unsettles me, and I try to ignore it. When we enter the outskirts of town, the spindly assistant to the town manager appears, running down the road toward us. I grow worried and wonder if we have done something wrong. At last he reaches us. Wheezing, he tells us to turn around, that the majority leader has been delayed, that the execution will have to be held tomorrow or the following day. The soldier grumbles.

"How will I know when?" I ask.

"We will send for you."

The assistant watches us start back toward the jail. As we do, I realize I am relieved. My muscles are sore, and I do not want to make a mistake. Also, I would prefer not to carry out an execution so soon after Lena's death. I only admit this to myself after learning of the delay.

At the jail, the soldier explains what has happened. The jailer, glaring at me, spits on the ground. He accepts the prisoner without a word.

The pot of chicken soup is still on the stove at the house, but I am not hungry. Inside I remove the sheet and blanket from the bed, tossing them onto the chest with the whetstone. I push the chest back into the corner. After putting on fresh clothes, I lie down. It is still light out. Eventually I fall asleep.

×

In the morning I look for Lena in her chair before I remember yesterday's events. With the shovel, I smooth the dirt over her grave. Then I gather stones to mark the border. It is difficult to believe she is no longer alive, that she will never again sit beside the window or laugh at something that happened in the market. I will miss her.

I go for a walk, following the road away from town, past farmhouses, then turning north into fields of young wheat. When I go far enough, there is only an endless skin of gold, and I almost forget everything.

Afterward I visit the jail to see if there is any news. The jailer stays inside his house when I call to him. The boy, playing with his toy in the yard, sneers at me. He says there has been no word about the execution. Then he adds, "You hit my father." His eyes dart toward me and away.

"I did not hit him," I reply. "I stopped him from beating a prisoner." I glance at Ear and Two, both seated in the corner of their cell. Ear is watching us.

"You cannot hit whoever you like," the boy says. His sneer disappears, and a look of fear crosses his face. After a moment he goes to sit on the bench. He meets my gaze again. I can see he is determined not to look away.

I stop myself from replying. The boy is merely defending his father.

On the walk home, I wonder if a visit to Emmer might improve my mood. I decide to wait a day or two before I see her.

When I come in sight of my house, I find the road blocked by four young boys. They have stones in their hands, more piled at their feet. One brings back his arm as I approach, and I lift my arm to shield myself. The hurled stone hits just below my wrist, and a dull pain spreads along my arm.

"Our friend almost died," shouts the thrower. He picks up another stone from the pile at his feet.

The jailer's son must have told the boys where I live. I glance at the farmer's house down the road. There is no one in sight. I turn back. "You attacked me first, remember?" My voice, much louder than the boy's, booms out over the road. I hope it will scare him. "I did not mean to hurt him."

"You think we're scared of you because you're the executioner?"

"Your friend is fine now. So leave me—"

A stone strikes me in the middle of the chest, knocking the wind out of me. Another hits me in the thigh, close to the groin. I show my back to my attackers, then crouch into a ball, with my arms around my head, to protect myself as best I can. It occurs to me that I can run, or that I can pick up some of the stones and defend myself, but maybe they are right: maybe I deserve to be punished. I feel a sharp pain in the back of my head.

×

When I open my eyes, it is night and I am lying in the road. A woman crouches on the shoulder, watching me. Though the moon is only a sliver in the sky, I see it is Lena.

"Look," she says, staring at me.

It does not surprise me to see her, or to hear her speak as she used to. Slowly I push myself up so that I am sitting on the ground. "I was attacked," I say.

"By children."

"What would you have had me do?"

She sniggers. "There is nothing you can do."

Gingerly I touch my head. It is tender, but there is no blood.

"After you lose your position," she continues, "you won't have enough money for your whore."

"Don't call her that," I say, and I am surprised by the strength in my voice. "You don't know—"

"Whore!"

I grit my teeth and feel a pain spread from the back of my head.

"If I were you, I would join the rebellion." She laughs. "They'll take you."

"I'm not going to listen to you anymore."

She hops toward me while still crouched on the ground, her hands in the dust. Then she cranes her neck forward. Her neck extends farther and farther and farther still. I wait for her to say something more, but she is silent.

When I wake, it is still night. I look around but I am alone. I turn over on my hands and knees and my body throbs with what feels like a hundred cuts. When I manage to stand, my vision blurs. I stumble home and drink from the well, then take the blanket from the top of the chest and sink onto the bed. Before I fall asleep, I think: if I die, it will be the jailer's boy who finds me.

It is at least late morning when I open my eyes again, because the sun has already risen above the windows. Every movement causes pain, so I lie still. Then my hunger grows and I force myself up, onto the edge of the bed. I manage to reach across to the table and take the two-thirds or so loaf of bread from under the bowl. I tear off a few big chunks and eat quickly. I grow tired and fall back asleep.

When I open my eyes, the jailer's boy stands in the doorway. The light in the house is a dull orange. Thinking the boy is from my mind, like Lena, I close my eyes. He begins talking. He talks and stops and talks and stops. I cannot understand him. I open my eyes.

"What do you want?" I ask.

"The town manager wants to see you."

"I'm sick." I close my eyes. When I open them later, he is still there. I remember that he told the boys how to find me, but I am too weak to feel anger. "Can you bring me some water?"

"You got what you deserve." He disappears. I close my eyes, but then I hear footsteps. The boy sets a full pail on the ground beside the head of the bed. From the table he takes a cup and fills it. He passes it to me and I drink, at first propping myself up on one elbow, then sitting up when I feel a sharp pain in my upper arm.

After a long a silence, he says, "There has been fighting in the countryside. My father says the majority leader will probably never come."

I shake my head and lie back down as he continues to talk. I fall asleep.

When I stir, I am alone. I stagger outside in the moonlight. Instead of going to the toilet, I empty my bladder onto the slope facing town. The steady stream of my urine is reassuring. When I return inside, I shut the door and then the windows. In the dark I almost fall over Lena's chair. I lie back on the bed.

I jerk up when I feel something move near the heel of bread at my side. What must be a mouse scurries off the bed. I hear it drop to the floor and see a dark spot cross the faint line of gray light at the bottom of the closed door. To protect the bread, I set it under the bowl on the table.

The next day I eat what is left of the mouse-nibbled loaf. My head feels better, but my body still aches, and I spend the day resting, and also the following day. The windows and door I leave closed. Only a little light comes in at their edges while the sun is up, so that it is always dark. Sleep comes and goes. At times I cannot tell if I am awake or dreaming, but at other times I can think clearly.

My fourth day in bed, my body is stiff, but the pain in my head has lessened, and my eyes no longer hurt when I go outside and look at something. I open the windows and door. Dirt covers the bed. I should clean it, but first I need something in my stomach. I have not eaten in two days. To my surprise, I find my money still in my pocket. I set off for the baker's shop on the west side of town.

As I walk, I remember that the town manager wants to speak with me. I do not feel ready to see him. If he has waited this long, he can wait a little longer.

The breeze feels good against my skin, and I am happy to be alive and well. I think of the gang of boys. Though I grow angry when I recall the stones raining down on me, I am glad they will not bother me anymore. As for the jailer's son, it is difficult for me to blame him.

On the walk back, I grow dizzy and sit down on the side of the road with the loaf in my hand. I wonder if Lena will appear while I wait for the spell to pass, but she does not. At home, I am surprised to realize that I do not miss her. Without her sitting in the chair, I feel more at ease. Almost like a new person.

The tomatoes in a bag in the corner are spotted and beginning to crumple into themselves, so I eat bread with just onion and a little oil. I cannot remember when food tasted so good. I wash the blanket and sheet and my clothes as best I can and hang them outside to dry, and I sweep the floor. Then I take *Histories of the New World* from the chest and lie naked on the bare bed. I open the book to one of my favorite parts.

This section tells of a people who rejected any notion of a past or future. They thought of time not as a circle or a line, but as a point. Previous events, from a child's birth to the destruction of a shelter by a storm, were thought to be like dreams, because they could mirror and even influence the present, but remained illusions. Memories were viewed as no more than creations of the mind, and if the memories of two or more individuals agreed, it was seen only as showing personal similarity. Death was without special status. When someone died, the body was left where it lay.

This view of the world shaped the language. In the native tongue, there was no way to describe something happening in the future, as in "I will go." Nor were there words like "tomorrow" or even "soon." When a trader tried to explain what he meant by "future," he was told that what is to come does not exist and so should not be discussed or named.

I guess it makes sense that this people thought in concrete ways. According to the book, emotions like hope and fear, and even love and hate, were tempered among them. Marriage did not exist, and while the mother or father usually cared for offspring, this did not always happen, and children wandered at will. Visitors expected disorder under this system, but the opposite was true, with individuals ending disputes through compromise. The goal of all agreements was to spread happiness.

When missionaries arrived in the area, the population was less than a thousand. After greeting their visitors, the people laughed at the promise of heaven as a reward but welcomed the idea of turning the other cheek. Eventually they were enslaved and died out in the mining camps at the center of the continent.

When I first came across this section, I was confused and went over it many times. Eventually I understood that this people considered the past and future to be without meaning. While this fascinated me, I thought there must be something I was missing.

Now, after rereading this section, I am struck by the possibility that one can believe only in the present. If there is no past, and no future, then I am completely free. I can forget about executions, about the town manager, about Lena. I can be with Emmer.

I look down at my naked body, still sore from its beating. Maybe I will feel strong enough tomorrow to see her.

Tomorrow. The future again. It is not so easy to escape.

Smiling, I continue reading. Occasionally I close my eyes and rest.

×

After waking late the next morning, I rise and cut myself a slice of bread. As I eat, I think again of the town manager, of the jail and the execution, and suddenly it seems clear to me that one day I will lose my position, that I will be cast aside by the town, that I will be forgotten and left to live out my days alone in this house. But I decide not to think of such things. I decide to live only in the present.

I go for a walk. South along the streets on the western edge of town to the stream. Then west, following the water with the sun against my back. My legs are not as steady as I would like, and I stop at the pool beneath the small waterfall. Sitting down, I listen to the water glide over the rocks and drop into the dark blue circle a few feet below. When a young couple, maybe teenagers, appear among the bushes on the other side, I slip away.

At nightfall I visit the brothel. Emmer is glad to see me, that I can tell from how she comes up and squeezes my arm. Her grip hurts, though I do not say so. After I pay Bersil and we go upstairs, she tries to push me onto the bed from behind. She is not strong enough. Wincing, I sit down slowly.

"What's wrong?" she asks.

I explain how I was attacked.

She laughs, a sound that begins as a loud cry and turns into wheezing. She only showed me her laugh after we had seen each other many times.

"What's so funny?" I ask, but I start to laugh with her despite the pain it sends down my side. My body shakes, and I laugh and laugh. Finally I grow quiet.

"They were only children!" she says.

"Children with stones."

"Why not fight back, or scare them away?"

“What if I hurt one of them?”

“But you hurt one before.”

“An accident.”

Her last wheeze fades. She sits down next to me and touches my head. “Does it still hurt?”

I shake my head.

She laughs again, briefly. “My brother, when he was young, tried to make me do everything exactly like him. Walking—this foot, then this foot, back straight, swing your arms. And eating—one bite, then chew, then take a small mouthful of water. And even laughing—open your mouth only this wide, not so loud, don’t suck the air into your stomach. Luckily he never tried to make me pee like him! Finally I had to tell him no more, that we’re not the same. You do things your way, and I do things mine.”

I consider her meaning. “You think I’m like your brother?”

“You’re nothing like my brother. I think that, if you were me, you would have done everything he said.”

I imagine myself as a little girl walking in step beside her brother. She is challenging me. “No,” I say. “No, I wouldn’t.”

“Lie down.”

I lie down crosswise on the bed, my feet resting on the floor.

She laughs again.

I realize what she has just done. I try to rise, but she crawls on top of me, and quickly I forget what I intended. I do not mention the aches in my body, the bruises that throb when she presses on me. There are moments when I feel like I might faint, when everything around me shifts and loses its clearness.

Afterward, while we lie together on the bed, I tell her about Lena. She is silent.

"Now there is enough room in my house for you," I say.

She pulls away from me. "I told you I don't want to leave here."

"I don't understand."

"Maybe accept that you cannot understand. I cannot understand why you like your work."

I think about this. I am not sure I do like my work.

"You can visit as much as you like," she adds.

"I don't always have enough money."

She is silent again. It is the silence that always seems to separate us. "What is that smell?"

"What smell?"

"You don't smell it? Burning. Smoke." She goes to a window. "Look."

I move to the window and stand beside her. Through the rows of slats I see, on the other side of the graveyard, flames rising from the compound shared by the garrison and jail. Figures move between the fire's light and the darkness. I smell the smoke hidden by the night.

"It must be the rebels," she says.

"How can you be sure?"

"What else? An accident?"

I hear a series of faint gunshots. The flames sprouting from the compound seem to move and yet to be completely still, and there is something both terrifying and exciting in them, in the possibility that they will destroy not only the garrison and jail but all of the town, the possibility that they will wipe away everything.

After a while, I say, "I should go to the jail."

She looks at me. "Let it burn. What do you care?"

"There are prisoners there," I say, thinking of Ear and Two. "What if they're hurt?"

"What does it matter? They will be executed anyway."

"And if there are no more executions? Anyway, maybe I can help stop the fire."

"Let others handle it."

"But I am the executioner."

She turns back toward the window, unwilling to argue with me any longer, it seems.

I am not sure I do care about the prisoners, or the jail. Maybe it is only the sight of the flames that draws me. "Come with me," I say as I dress. "It will be better up close."

"You know I can't leave while I'm working," she replies. She lies on the bed. "You should stay here. What if the rebels are taking control of the town?"

I finish dressing. Never before have I imagined that the rebels might win. Who would they have me execute? The town manager? The jailer?

“They will not be friendly with someone who killed so many of their comrades,” she adds.

She’s right, of course, and her words make me pause. “But why should they blame me? I only do as I’m told.”

She smiles.

“They are probably gone by now. I will just go and take a look.” I stand at the side of the bed, not moving.

“Go if you want,” she says.

I return to the window and look out again at the flames in the night sky, at the figures scurrying about like ants. What am I so worried about? If they do take the town, it is better to go to them on my own and convince them I did not choose who to execute. I glance at the clock by the bed. Not much of my hour remains. I say goodbye to Emmer. It is only as I am walking out of the brothel that I realize what her smile meant earlier. *I only do as I’m told.* But now am I doing what I’m told?

Instead of taking the road back through town, I cut through the graveyard. I feel dew on the grass through my sandals. I forgot how damp the night was. There seems to be little chance of the fire spreading.

The coal lumps of the hills, darker than the sky, rise on my right, while on my left the town lights flicker, and in front of me the fire grows brighter until I can read the writing on the gravestones at my feet. I walk as I usually do, straight backed, with long, even strides, as if I am taking a night stroll.

As I near the road, I pass two bodies in the sheepskins of the hill people. They lie sprawled and blood-spattered on the ground.

By the time I reach the garrison walls, sweat is trickling down my sides and back. I stop at the open gate, beside one of the posts topped by the army's diamond-shaped symbol, its metal surface glinting, at its center two birds joined by a shared wing.

The flames no longer seem motionless. They whip back and forth, feeding on the storehouse in the far corner, by the wall that separates the garrison and the jail. The garrison itself is so brightly lit from the fire that I can see every detail, from the open eyes of the bodies scattered on the dirt, to the speckled texture of the stucco walls, to the water hurled into the air by the soldiers hurrying to and from the well in the center of the courtyard.

"What are you doing here?"

A soldier is pointing his musket at me. It takes a moment for me to reply, and he repeats himself.

"I was walking past," I say, "and I saw the fire."

"How do I know you're—"

"That's the executioner," says another soldier.

"Is it?" He looks at my face. "Oh, right. Get on then. You can't be here."

He gestures with his musket toward town, and so I begin walking down the road. I glance back a few times. Soon I see he has stopped watching me. I hurry out of sight around the corner, moving to the jail entrance. There is no sign of the jailer or his boy, or of anyone else. Through the doorway in the wall separating the jail and garrison, I can see the back of the soldier who questioned me. I cross to the cells so he will not see me if he turns around.

Flames rise over the wall at the end of the cells, lighting up the jail as clearly as the garrison. The high wooden roof above the bars has burned. All that remains are charred bits of timber and ash fallen the twenty feet to the ground. Among the rubble, the prisoner Two is slumped forward on the ground. Ear is nowhere to be seen.

I look behind me to see if we are still alone. Only then do I notice water dripping from the roof of the jailer's house. He must have doused it to stop the fire from spreading.

I move closer to the cell. With each step the heat from the flames on the other side of the wall grows more intense. The bars of the cell are pitched forward, the door bent, the lock warped and broken.

"Two," I say, but he does not stir, and I realize that "Two" is not his actual name, that, in any case, he probably cannot hear me over the roar of the fire. Ear wanted me to execute Two because he was sick, and the doctor made light of Lena's death because, in his words, she was not leading a rich life. But such things do not matter. These people are still with us. I reach out and pull on the warm bars of the cell door. There is no movement.

I pull again, straining with my sore muscles, until the door slides out a few feet, the bottom dragging on the ground. I squeeze inside and haul Two out by his arms, his back to me. He seems to be breathing. When I try to stand him up in the middle of the courtyard, he falls back onto the ground. I cannot even make him sit. Laying him on his back, I shout his name. Pus rings his swollen eyelids.

"What are you doing?"

I turn. The jailer and his boy stand at the jail entrance. I ask, "Where have you been?"

"Where have I been?" the jailer repeats, looking at his boy in pretend confusion. "Don't worry about where I've been. What are you doing with the prisoner?"

"He was in the cell. He looked hurt."

"You can't release a prisoner from the cell!"

"He could die."

"That's no concern of yours. Why are you here?"

"I was taking a walk when I saw the flames."

"Suspicious, isn't it?" he says to the boy. "He's lucky if we don't report him, isn't he?" He looks back at me. "Is there anything else?"

I look around. "Where is Ear?"

"Where is Ear?" the jailer repeats in a mocking tone. "Dead."

There is a silence as this sinks in. "How did he die?"

"He cut himself."

It dawns on me that something is wrong. The jailer is lying. "You killed him?"

"Would it matter if I did? You were supposed to execute him."

The boy looks from me to his father, and I consider the jailer's words. It is true that Ear was going to be executed. But his execution was delayed.

"Anything else?" the jailer says, loudly.

"You should not have killed him."

"Who says I killed him? Now get out of here."

I look again at Two. I cannot tell if he is breathing now. The jailer is shouting at me. "Get out of here!" he says, advancing.

"You cannot order me around."

"Yes, I can. Anyone can order you around!"

Then he is sprawled on his back, bleeding from the nose. I have struck him. The boy is waving a small knife. "Leave," he says.

"I will report you," the jailer shouts from the ground, touching his face.

My body is shaking. I take one step toward them. The boy does not move. Then I turn and hurry home, glancing back at the jail and the flames to see if I am being followed. Though I am afraid of the step I have taken, a sense of freedom, pure and exhilarating, washes over me.

In the morning, I stumble quickly out of bed. From the garden I see last night's blaze has been extinguished. Everything in town seems as usual, at least from where I stand.

After eating the last of the bread, I check the stones around Lena's grave. I debate whether to add more stones but decide against doing so. Then I take a long walk, winding my way through the wheat fields to the west. The soreness in my limbs and chest lingers. I try to focus on each step, but an image of the jailer lying on the ground, his nose bleeding, pushes its way into my mind. I worry that I will be punished for striking him, for letting Two out of the cell.

On the way back, as I turn the bend in the road, I spot the jailer's son at the edge of Lena's grave. I call out to him: "What do you want?"

"The town manager asked for you. He said it's urgent."

I remain silent. Has the jailer reported my actions?

"Come quickly," the boy says. He hesitates, as if he wants to say more. Then he jogs down the road.

Instead of starting for town, I go inside and sit at the table. I have always done my duty. If I am in trouble, if the town manager thinks I have violated one rule or another, he will have to wait.

In the afternoon, the breeze carries sounds of sawing and hammering from the direction of town. Probably people are busy repairing damage from the attack. I am reluctant to visit one of the bakers to buy more bread, and I pass the rest of the day in bed without eating. I re-read the section from *Histories*. I still like the idea that only the present has meaning, but I am less and less sure how to make sense of this in my own life.

×

In the morning I sleep later than I intend. After I step outside, I see that there are more cooking fires than usual: thin columns of smoke crowd the skyline. The faint clatter of construction continues.

With my stomach groaning, I risk a visit to the baker on the west side of town. The trip passes without incident, although I see more people than usual talking with each other. They pay no attention to me. Returning home, I devour a third of the loaf. My thoughts flit about. Part of me wants to see what the town manager has to say, but the other part warns me to stay away. Feeling restless, I go for a walk, threading my way to the stream and dipping my feet in the chill water. After a while, I start back.

When I turn off the road toward my house, a soldier emerges from inside. Two more appear behind him. Unlike the soldiers from the garrison, their uniforms have three red stars along each arm.

"Time to go," the first soldier tells me in an accent I have never heard. His tone is neither friendly nor hostile.

"Where?" I say.

"Where do you think?"

At the thought that I am going to be punished for striking the jailer, that I may lose my position or even be thrown in jail, my fists clench and I plant my feet. Then it occurs to me that the jailer's offense is greater than my own. He killed Ear. If I explain this to the town manager, he will certainly be lenient with me. After thinking this through a second time, I start toward the road, expecting the soldiers to follow me.

"Are you going to use your hands?" another soldier says, cackling.

I stop and turn. "What do you mean?"

"Are you going to strangle them with your big strong hands?" He is laughing harder now, though he is the only one laughing.

"Get your axe," the first soldier says.

"My axe?"

"Hurry up. We're supposed to be there soon."

An execution, I realize. They are asking me to carry out my duty. I am confused but also relieved: I am not in trouble. Maybe the majority leader has arrived in town. Maybe that is why there were so many cooking fires. After a moment, I collect my axe from inside.

The soldiers remain silent while we walk. As we near the jail, I grow more and more uneasy. On the one hand, there are my responsibilities as the executioner. On the other, there is what Emmer said. I only do as I am told. I would like to show her, and myself, that I am capable of doing whatever I please.

More soldiers with the star uniform stand in the corners of the jail courtyard. The jailer, his cheek bruised, scowls at me from the bench. I do not see Two anywhere, but new prisoners fill the now roofless cells. As I watch, the jailer's son helps his father shackle three of them. When one resists, the jailer strikes him with his baton, once on the hip, once on the back of the thigh. He crumples briefly to the ground. The jailer prods the three prisoners until they climb onto the wagon. The boy steals a look at me.

"What happened to Two?" I ask.

"Dead," the jailer says without facing me.

"How did he die?"

"The same way we all do." He glares at me, then moves away.

Two of the prisoners are middle-aged and graying. The third, the prisoner who resisted the jailer, is only a boy, though he is as tall as a man. I have never executed a boy before. I think about this. From the vantage of the present, all three are the same: alive. Yet the boy has a long life in front of him.

"He is so young," I say.

"He is one of the leaders."

"How do you know?"

The jailer does not answer, and soon the wagon is trundling down the main road to town with an escort of five soldiers, and I must hurry to catch up. As I follow, balancing the axe on my shoulder, the jailer shouts, "What a halfwit!" Then he erupts into laughter.

The soldiers accompanying the wagon glance at me but say nothing, and my face flushes. As we walk, I think of Ear and Two. I tell myself I am doing my duty, but I grow angry when I recall the jailer's insult, when I think of the expectation that I will do whatever I am told.

One of the soldiers interrupts my thoughts by shouting. The young prisoner has taken a seat on the wagon, and the soldier orders him to stand. When the prisoner does not respond, the soldier jabs him with his bayonet, drawing a pinprick of blood above his knee. This gets him to his feet. The wagon rocks back and forth, and the three prisoners must focus on keeping their balance.

After a while, I advance to one side, behind one of the soldiers, and say to the young prisoner: "How old are you?"

He jerks his head to the side. Then he spits on me, and the gob lands atop my head. The soldier who stabbed him rams the butt of his musket into the boy's shins. The boy winces but manages to remain upright. He stares with hatred at the soldier, then at me. The soldier fixes me with a strange look.

"Swine," the prisoner says softly. Whether he is speaking to me or the soldier is unclear. His voice is high and immature.

"What did you say?" the soldier says to the boy, slamming the butt into his shins again. This time the prisoner falls onto the floor of the wagon. Slowly he pushes himself back to his feet.

With my free hand I try to wipe away the saliva. I only end up mixing it into my tangle of hair. Yet I do not feel angry at the prisoner. Instead I am embarrassed to be executing someone so young.

The jailer's boy follows fifty or so feet behind us. When I turn and stop, he stops too. The prisoner who spit on me is probably only a few years older.

In town, people stand along the streets and inside doorways to watch as we pass. I even spy the garlic seller from the market. She waves. I hesitate before raising a hand in greeting. It is the first time anyone has waved at me on my way to an execution. At the square, the crowd must part for us to enter. I see then that the platform for the executions has been raised. Now it is a lofty seven or eight feet above the ground. Also, in front of the town hall, a viewing area has been built for the occasion, with seats covered by a tent. In the shade of this tent, the town manager sits and chats with men in bright clothes. The majority leader must be among them.

The wagon shakes violently as it rolls over the flagstones of the square. About halfway to the platform, a back wheel gets caught in a gap. After trying to force the horse forward, the soldiers and I struggle to lift up the wheel, but by then it is wedged between two stones, and we cannot pry it out. The crowd watches, talking among themselves. The gaze of so many townspeople unnerves me. In their faces I recognize disdain.

Without warning, I feel a blow to my stomach. The axe falls from my shoulders, its butt clanging against the flagstones. The crowd roars. The boy prisoner has attacked a soldier and then me, lashing out in an attempt at escape. Two soldiers subdue him and force him up to the platform. There they unshackle him and tie his hands to the metal rings protruding from the middle of three blocks. One of the soldiers bludgeons him with the butt of his musket. Then he and his companion force his head into the hollow. They use a rope to ensure he cannot move. The other soldiers escort the two older prisoners. These men, lean and tan, walk up the stairs with an attempt at dignity. The attempt strikes me as laughable, but I am in no mood to laugh.

After the soldiers tie down all three prisoners, they abandon the platform. One says to me, "Get on with it."

The crowd grows quiet, and I do not move right away. Everyone's attention is on me. Is this what it feels like to be in control? To wield power?

I remain motionless, wondering what will happen if I turn and leave, if I follow my own whim. Then I heave the axe back onto my shoulder and start toward the platform. I am worried that I will fall as I climb the steep steps, so I angle forward. Once I reach the top, there is the loud call of a candied almond vendor, then a low murmuring. The boy prisoner is weeping. The whimpering sounds he makes are too faint, I think, for the crowd to hear. At such moments I have learned to steel myself, but today I am anxious for the execution to be finished. I advance to the prisoner on the eastern end of the platform. From there I look around the square, at the graceful olive trees lining its edges, at the sharp spire of the church, at the tent with its seated figures underneath, at the countless faces watching me. The murmuring in the crowd continues. I feel repelled by the spectacle I am enacting, by the people waiting to be entertained. Yet I must go on. The prisoner's muscles are rigid. There is no reason to wait any longer. I lift the axe and bring it down. The prisoner's head rolls onto the platform and blood spurts across the wood, as it always does. The crowd barely stirs, but when I turn, I think I hear a few jeers. I start toward the middle prisoner, the boy. He is still weeping. I have heard many prisoners weep, but I do not think I can bear this. I pass him, continuing to the other end of the platform. The iron scent of blood fills my nostrils. There is also something else. The odor of bodily waste. The prisoner on the western end seems almost as if he is asleep, his body relaxed and completely still. I avoid looking at the crowd. I lift the blade high into the air, as high as I can. Then I bring it down and the head rolls and blood blossoms across the platform, finding its way onto my pants, onto my sandals and feet. There are a few cheers but also, unmistakably, taunts. I close my eyes and remind myself that I am doing my duty.

As I move to the middle block, a scraping sound follows me. I am dragging the axe. I lift the spattered blade over my shoulder. I have forgotten a cloth to wipe it. I try to keep my focus, to live only in the present, but more than anything I want to escape the present. The young prisoner's soft weeping continues. I peer down at his thin neck, at the life I am charged with ending. A whispering surges around me.

"How old are you?" I ask the boy again.

His weeping grows louder, becomes audible, I am sure, to the onlookers. I imagine the moment when I will be done with this execution. I gaze at the crowd and find that I loathe them. Then I lift the axe high into the air, as high as I can. As I scan the people around the platform, I see Emmer and Lena standing a few feet apart, separated by young children. Lena is laughing. Then I blink and they are gone, and there is a screaming. It is the crowd. No. It is the prisoner. He is screaming into the block.

I have missed his neck, making a gash in his shoulder. The wound overflows and blood rushes onto the platform. The blade sticks partly out of the block's side. Horrified, I quickly free the axe. I bring it down again, but my arms lack steadiness. This time it nicks the spot where the shoulder meets the neck, driving mostly into the wood. The prisoner's screams grow louder. I hear laughing, I think, from the crowd. Anger gives me a sudden burst of strength, and when I bring the axe down a third time, the prisoner's head rolls onto the platform, then continues rolling until it falls onto the flagstones with a sickening thud.

When I turn toward the town hall, I see some of the well-dressed figures from the tent hurrying away, the town manager following them. I survey the faces in the crowd. There are jokes and more taunts.

My throat is tight with nausea, and I am not sure what to do next. I cannot believe I failed to provide the prisoner with a clean death. I feel disgusted by his execution, by all of the executions.

A band of young boys approaches and begins chanting. Are they the same boys who attacked me before? I cannot tell. Slowly I make out their words. "Chop! Chop! Chop! Chop!"

"Leave me alone," I tell them, but their chanting only grows louder. "Leave me alone!" They continue, encouraged by my reaction.

Dropping the axe, I stagger down the platform's stairs and hurry home. What remains of the crowd parts for me, and though the children follow me for a ways, soon they grow tired of their sport. On the outskirts of town I notice my shirt is smeared with blood.

I undress completely at the well beside my house and pour water over my head again and again, until my skin almost feels clean. Then I wash my clothes and hang them to dry. I put on fresh clothes. There is bread, but I am not hungry. I lie in bed, unable to fall asleep. I have left my axe. I have also failed to cart the bodies to the graveyard.

At nightfall, I catch a whiff of something rotting. I wonder if I am imagining the smell, but it grows stronger. I step outside. After scanning my surroundings, I notice the pot of chicken soup I cooked for Lena. I left it on the stove. I open the lid, and a stench of decaying flesh floods out. After more than a week, the soup has turned putrid. Holding my breath, I carry the pot and empty the contents onto the far end of the slope that descends to the neighboring wheat field. I leave the empty pot at the edge of the garden. Then I go to Lena's grave. It is like before. I lie on my back on the oval patch of earth, with my limbs extended over the stones, and gaze up at the stars. I fall asleep there.

×

Long after the sun has risen, I wake and crawl into the shade on the north side of the house. I feel nauseous and am not sure what to do with myself.

While sitting against the wall, I go over yesterday's events. It occurs to me that, if I am capable of a lapse, an error, like yesterday's, the legislators in the capital may be right: executions may be inhumane. But isn't error possible in other things too? Isn't it possible, for example, to jail someone who is innocent? And does this mean taking prisoners is inhumane?

There is something else. The feeling that overcame me during the execution. A feeling of disgust with the town and my duties. Maybe it is for the best if I lose my position, if the town casts me aside. Yet, if this comes to pass, I have no idea what I will do.

I remain seated on the ground for much of the day. Then, in the afternoon, I lie on the bed. I expect someone to come and tell me to bring the bodies to the graveyard or collect my axe, but no one comes. The following day it is the same. I try to read from *Histories*, but now it is difficult for me to focus on the words. On the third day, I venture to the baker's shop on the west side of town. He has a sly smile when he sells me a loaf. Otherwise everything is as usual. More days pass without anyone coming or sending word for me to visit the town manager. I begin to suspect that I have already been cast aside, that the town manager has decided to forget me.

I ask myself: is this not what I should want?

After debating the best course of action, I buy some tomato seeds from the grocery and plant them in the garden. This makes me feel as if I am doing something useful, and I think of the market. I decide to try selling herbs again. Though I sell nothing the first day I return, I convince myself that I may carve out a living if I persist. I go back on the following days. After one week, business picks up ever so slightly. I am an oddity among all the women sellers, and some people visit me for this reason alone. Most of the sellers shun me, but the garlic seller remains friendly, and I begin to believe in the possibility of a continued life in this town. Then I think of Emmer, of my last meeting with her, and I wonder if there is any point. She will always live at the brothel, and I will always have to pay to see her.

One morning, before I set out for the market, the jailer's boy appears at the house.

"The town manager has asked to see you," he announces from the door.

There is a silence. Without looking at him, I say, "I will go soon."

"I'm to wait with you until you go, and walk with you there."

"But I have things to do."

"You have nothing to do."

It is true, of course, that I have nothing to do, nothing that cannot be put off. But I water the garden anyway, and check Lena's grave to make sure the stones around its edges are still in place. He shadows me. I am reminded of the boy I executed.

"You must be worried," he says. "They say a man from the capital, a man in the audience, became sick, and that the town manager promised to punish you. My father, he says that, if he were you, he would leave town. That's what he says."

I find that I am not afraid of what will happen. There is no point putting it off. We set out for the town square together, the boy keeping a few feet behind me no matter how slow my pace. When I ask him about the jail, he mumbles a vague reply. I feel sure I will lose my position, and I grow excited at this prospect. As we near the town hall, an idea occurs to me. Maybe I can convince Emmer to leave with me for the New World. She enjoyed the stories I told her from *Histories*. After saving some of what I make at the market, we can escape there together.

Pleased by this prospect, I quicken my pace. At the town hall's giant wooden doors, the boy stops and clears his throat. He says, "My father was right. I never should have helped you."

I turn to look at him. Despite his spiteful words, I see the same old look of fear on his face.

Upstairs I wait in the reception room. I can hear the town

manager talking to someone inside his office. Maybe it is the new executioner. Though I cannot make out any words, the murmuring makes me queasy. I move to the bookshelf against the wall to distract myself. I think: *I only do as I'm told*. I stare at the individual books on the shelf in front of me, the many-colored spines, the letters of different sizes and types. Without reading any of the titles, I take one and slip it under the back of my shirt, against my waist, so that my belt helps hold it in place. In fact, I do not especially care about the book. I only want to take something that is the town manager's.

Footsteps sound inside, and the door opens. I turn to see the jailer swagger out of the office. So, he will be the new executioner. But he cannot handle an axe.

After pausing to smirk at me, the jailer leaves and the town manager enters the reception room. "What are you doing?" he asks, scanning the bookshelf.

I move back into the center of the room, staying silent and keeping my hands behind me so the book does not fall. Soon it becomes clear to him that I am not going to reply.

"I was very upset with your performance the other day. *Par fornir*, to accomplish—and what was accomplished? The majority leader called it a mockery, do you understand? I want to know what happened."

I feel my mouth go dry. Anyway, I have nothing to say.

"Have you no defense?"

I shake my head.

"Well, I understand your wife is sick, I understand that. And so, because of that and because of other events and because of my own personal generosity, I am willing to overlook this mishap."

After some time, the town manager smiles.

"That's right. I am in a good mood. I'll tell you why. The attack by the rebels has eclipsed your failure. The premier is sending us more soldiers, more money—more than ever before. We will build roads, improve our market, make our bridges the envy of the southern regions. Maybe we will even add a fountain! To be sure, bolstering our defenses is also important, but what can those rebels accomplish? They are too disorganized, too poorly armed." He laughs again and waits for me to respond. "Also, there is another development, one that directly affects you."

Here it comes, I think.

"In part because of our little performance—in fact, it may be largely due to our little performance, though I remind you that officially it never occurred—Parliament has decided that all executions will now be effected by a new, more humane method, one that makes death quicker, cleaner, more painless. A machine, you see. It has only recently been invented. They are sending us one from the capital, as well as a technician to show you how to use it. I have never seen the machine, but they say it relies on needles. One goes through the spine, others through the chest. Which means no axe. You strap in the prisoner, move a lever, that's all."

I wonder if I have understood him correctly.

"And you will be busy. After the recent attack, there are more than enough prisoners. You must have seen them at the jail."

I contemplate this. "I am still the executioner?"

He clenches his teeth and smooths his sheet of hair with both hands. "Why yes. Who else? Who else would I find for such a job in times such as these? But I warn you—don't embarrass me again. I'll send for you when the machine arrives." He stares at me with an indignant expression, his lip curled. Then, before I can think of anything more to say, he disappears into his office, shutting the door behind him.

For a while I remain standing in the reception room, going over the town manager's words in my mind. Then I take out the book and descend the stairs. In the shade around the corner from the town hall's front doors, I lean against the wall.

I still have my position, I think. Not only that, but I will have to use this new machine. The town manager expects me to be happy about this, I realize. He expects me to be happy for a chance to do a better job.

I feel dizzy, and so I close my eyes. Little by little the unsteadiness fades. It occurs to me that it will be easier to save money with an executioner's salary. If I am careful, soon I should have enough to buy passage to the New World, enough for Emmer and me to establish new lives there.

I consider this plan. To my surprise, I find that I begin laughing. My laughter grows louder and louder and louder still. I wait until the fit passes. Then, frowning, I start the long walk home.

Thanks to the writing communities at Florida State University and the University of Nevada, Las Vegas. Special thanks to Skip Horack, Daniel LoPilato, Richard Wiley and Maile Chapman for reading early drafts of this novella.

I owe thanks to my parents for their support and encouragement over the years. And to MC for her help with everything and for believing in me.

Clancy McGilligan grew up in Milwaukee and has worked as a journalist in the U.S. and abroad. His writing has appeared in publications such as *Slice Magazine*, *Sycamore Review*, *Columbia Journal*, *Santa Monica Review*, *USA Today*, *The Christian Science Monitor* and *Film International*.